About the author

Lorraine Turnbull wanted to be a farmer since she was five years old. In her mid-forties, she uprooted herself and her family and moved to a run-down one acre smallholding in Cornwall. She retrained as a teacher, worked as a Skills Co-ordinator for The Rural Business School, and started commercial cider making in 2010.

In 2014 she won the Cornwall Sustainability Awards Best Individual category, and successfully removed the Agricultural Occupancy Condition from her home. She moved to France in 2017 and her first book was published in May 2019.

Other books by the author

The Sustainable Smallholders Handbook (2019)
Sustainable Smallholding (2020)
Living off the Land: My Cornish Smallholding Dream (2020)
Mum's the Word (2021)
How to Live the Good Life in France (2nd edition 2022)

Connect with Lorraine:
Facebook https://www.facebook.com/
LorraineTurnbullAuthor/

Twitter @LorraineAuthor

Instagram lorraineauthor

YouTube Channel: Lorraine Turnbull Smallholder & Author

Murder at the Moulin

Lorraine Turnbull

Copyright

This is a work of fiction and the characters portrayed in it are the work of the author's imagination. Any real locations are used in a fictitious manner.

The moral right of the author has been asserted. All rights reserved. No part of this publication may be reproduced, stored in a retrieval system or recorded by any means, without prior written permission from the publisher.

Copyright © 2022 by Lorraine Turnbull

Fat Sheep Press, 46300 Milhac, France.

ISBN 978-1-7396072-0-3

Dedicated to my husband.

Chapter 1

Simon Parker left the *notaire*'s office armed with a bag of keys belonging to the dilapidated watermill in St Honoré, together with the ominous warning that his purchase may cause some unpleasantness by a minority of the villagers.

Although it was only eleven in the morning, the air shimmered as he opened the door to his pickup, releasing a burst of heat sufficient to bake a cake. He dumped the bulging folder of newly acquired documents onto the passenger seat, and held the door open to allow the heat to dissipate; fleetingly comparing this hot, blue-sky April day with the wintry showers he'd left behind in Bristol. The sunlight was blinding and he quickly donned his sunglasses, before sitting in what effectively was a mobile sauna. Thank God he wasn't wearing shorts, he thought as the heat from the pickup's seats burned through his chinos.

The plane trees that lined the small private car park had been severely pruned and provided no shade at this time of year, but he wasn't complaining. After a lifetime of British weather, the thought of proper seasons added to the excitement of his new project and life as a soon-to-be single man of good fortune living in one of the most beautiful areas of France.

He'd stumbled across the village quite by accident at the start of the year when he'd escaped the depressing thought of an English New Year as a newly-separated man, and found himself driving south through rural France. After a damp and chilly night in a *chambre d'hôtes* in Rouen, he headed further south; searching for something that didn't remind him of dreary winter. After getting sidetracked just south of Limoges, he found himself driving down the pretty Vezere Valley, and arrived in St Honoré. He'd pulled up on a small road outside the church and opened the map lying on the passenger seat, trying to decide the best route to drive further south and that was when he noticed the for sale sign on the small wall next to his car; the sign that changed his life.

***

The purchase had been spontaneous, which had somewhat surprised him, and he now faced an uphill struggle to reverse the reclamation by the land of the centuries old watermill in the quintessential Dordogne village, population 285. The transaction had been relatively quick, and with no alternative but to carry on with his spur-of-the-moment plan, he was now the owner of a dilapidated mill that was, in estate-agent parlance, *full of character and promise*.

Leaving the keys and the paperwork in the car, he walked the few yards to the *boulangerie*. His stomach rumbled, and he decided to kill two birds with one stone; pick up some bread and croissants and introduce himself to the no-doubt nosy inhabitants.

The door was open and a mouth-watering smell of fresh baked bread and pastries wafted out on the warm air. He by-passed the small scruffy sleeping dog at the door and took his place in the queue, waiting behind a plump matriarch with an enormous shopping bag. She seemed to be buying enough for a small army, and left with a bulging bag and a curious stare.

The pretty brunette behind the counter had a smear of flour on her cheek, but somehow it added to her charm, and Simon, in his halting French politely asked for two baguettes and two croissants. As she piled them into a bag for him, he introduced himself.

'I'm Simon Parker,' he smiled, 'I've just bought the old mill, so I thought I'd come and say hello.'

8

'I know who you are,' she said in English. 'I speak English. *Everyone* knows the name of Simon Parker, the Englishman who has bought *le vieux moulin* and everyone wants to know if you are to be a summer visitor or if you will stay all year round.'

Somewhat surprised at the directness of the introduction, Simon forced a smile, 'I'm intending to apply for residency,' he said crisply, 'but the mill needs a considerable amount of work before I can actually live there.'

'Obviously,' she smiled politely whilst rolling her dark brown eyes. She was pretty in a way that some girls are, but more so; and without a speck of make-up. Simon had to concentrate hard to keep to the point.

'Would you know if there is anywhere close-by in the village that I could rent a room for a month or so?'

She arched a perfect eyebrow and immediately shouted out of the door in French; and the large woman with the bag stuffed with bread reappeared instantly, as if; Simon suspected, she had been eavesdropping outside.

'This is Madame Cholet, she rents a room and may even cook, if you like French food,' she said by way of introduction.

The older woman smiled, 'Bonjour Monsieur.' Her quick dark eyes appraised him and he rewarded her interest with a broad smile.

'Enchanté Madame,' Simon returned, 'Je recherché une chambre pour un mois, s'il vous plait.'

Madame beamed, and they shook hands.

'Her house is just a short walk, so you can leave your car and go see if it is agreeable,' the brunette explained, stretching out her hand to take the money. Simon handed over a crisp note and smiled, 'If I need to know anything else, I'll come and ask you first.'

'Yes, I know everything, *and* everybody; and of course, everyone will want to know all about you too.' He was very aware of the intense scrutiny he was under by both women and wondered if he should show them his teeth to complete their visual examination, but he resisted the urge to be flippant and continued politely.

'Well, after Madame Cholet shows me her room, I'm going to the *mairie* to put in my *déclaration préalable* for the work on the mill, so you can tell them all straight from the horse's mouth.'

She wrinkled her nose, 'A *horse's* mouth?'

'Directly from me,' he explained with a smile. 'Thank you again, Miss..?'

'Émilie Fournier.'

***

Madame Cholet led him to a small two-storey stone house, opposite the church. Up a narrow set of wooden stairs was a small bedroom, dominated by a dark oak double bed, a wardrobe and a window overlooking the square. The tiny *salle de douche* was next to the bedroom and Simon managed somehow to hide his disappointment. It was only for a short time, after all, he promised himself.

They agreed a price for the month, which Simon paid in cash and she handed him a key. Her husband was a stone mason and left early for work, so Simon must be quiet if he came in late at night, breakfast was at seven, and he could eat with them in the evening if he warned her in the morning. He would eat with them tonight at seven sharp, she informed him with a wagging finger.

He returned to his pickup and transferred his bags to the room, assuring himself that although it wasn't the Ritz, it was handy and cheap. Then he visited the *mairie*, who had already been alerted by the village bush telegraph, and pored over his plans and application, explaining that he had already detailed his plans to the various heritage organisations.

Delighted that the dilapidated building would soon be an attractive feature in the village, the *maire*; through his English speaking colleague, assured Simon that they would do all they could to assist him, and wished him *bon courage*.

***

Finally he arrived at the mill, and took a long drink of water from his water bottle. A walk round to refresh his memory proved necessary, because when he had briefly viewed the mill in January, the vegetation was dead, and the trees bare. Now, new life and thick vegetation made the property almost unrecognisable. Acacia trees towered in the woodlands, filling the air with a sweet scent, and the grass was knee-high. Before he could begin to tame the wilderness and expose the building, his immediate need was somewhere to store all his tools. An inspection of the stone barn adjoining the mill revealed that as it was reasonably watertight, he only needed to repair the stiff and creaking door, and add a lock. He changed into his shorts and a tee-shirt and began to strip off the old hinges and lock. Soon after, the chiming of the church bells announced mid-day and he realised with a groan that he'd have to stop; the archaic rules forcing workers to stop using any power tools until after the two-hour traditional lunch break meant he couldn't make any noise.

He decided to take a walk to the *Salamandre* bar; opposite the mill, and see if he could get some food; and was greeted with nods and *bonjours* from the scattering of people already sitting down for the main meal of the day.

His waitress presented him with the *menu du jour*; terrine de campagne, poulet basquais and a choice of dessert, alongside an offer of *un petit pichet de vin rose ou rouge*, which he declined.

A few minutes later, the patron himself arrived with the terrine and a basket of bread and introduced himself as Henri, 'The wine is included in the price of the meal, so we will keep your wine in the bottle until you come *ce soir;* this evening. Welcome to St Honoré and *bon appétit*.'

Lunch was necessarily leisurely, after all there was no rush to return to the mill, and the service was timed to allow the diners to relax with their enjoyment of the food. Finally, around half past one, he paid and walked back to the mill, passing the *boulangerie* where Émilie was weeding the small, pretty garden surrounding the building. She stood briefly to acknowledge him, and watched him walk past. Quite good-looking, if you liked your men fair and muscular, she mused, and wondered; just like all her bakery customers had asked, when Mrs Parker would be arriving.

***

By mid-afternoon, the door was swinging freely and was sporting a brand-new shiny lock. Simon began to unload the trailer he had brought with him from his old home in Bristol, and stacked the tools along the rear wall of the shed. The ride-on mower was then unloaded, and checked over. Tomorrow he'd need to get fuel and attempt to give the overgrown meadow a cut, but for now, the brush-cutter would reduce the height of the grass to a height the mower could just about manage. Beginning just outside what was to become the mill front door, he strimmed a path around the building and then out in ever-widening arcs. He uncovered some old agricultural implements as he worked, and more than a few discarded glass bottles, which he piled up, but he realised he was enjoying himself, as he savoured the heat on his back and the smell of mint filling his nostrils.

As the sun began to dip, he stopped working, replaced the tools and the mower in the shed, locked up and walked to Madame Cholet's house, where her husband introduced himself briefly. 'Philippe', he said offering an elbow in greeting as he washed his hands and arms outside from a tap in the wall.

Simon followed suit, and then climbed the stairs to wash properly in the tiny *salle de douche*. He stripped his sweaty work clothes off and stepped under the shower, and was immediately disappointed. The water dribbled weakly from

12

the ancient shower and Simon contorted his large frame under
the weak dribble of lukewarm water, whilst trying to avoid
the touch of the plastic shower curtain. He emerged a few
minutes later to roughly towel-dry his short fair hair before
dressing in fresh clothes and returning downstairs to eat with
the Cholet's. Monsieur Cholet was a man of few words, and
simply passed the bread, water and plates to Simon. Madame
spooned large portions of *blanquette de veau* and rice onto
their plates and poured cold rosé wine for them. They ate well,
and afterwards, Philippe gestured to Simon with a jerk of his
head, 'Le Salamander?'

Simon thanked Madame for the meal and followed Philippe
out to walk the short distance to the bar.

As the evening was chilly, the few customers were sitting
inside the tiny, rustic bar, some sitting with a *pastis*, but more
with the local beverage of beer with a healthy dose of *picon*
liqueur to keep out the cold.

Philippe introduced Simon to the incumbents with a general
wave of his hand, and the patron, Henri shook his hand, and
passed him the rosé wine he'd declined at lunchtime. Without
being asked he poured Philippe a beer, and helped himself to a
pastis, pouring a small amount of water into the glass, turning
the glass an opaque dirty cream colour.

Simon sat and his eyes wandered around the interior of the
bar. It obviously hadn't been decorated in decades, and the
walls were covered in yellowing old photographs and posters
advertising local events. The ceiling was stained with years
of tobacco smoke, and the furniture looked like it had been
randomly salvaged at local *vide greniers,* but the glasses were
clean and the shelves were spotless.

An old man with a black Salvador Dali moustache sat
brooding silently in the back corner, nursing a glass of red
wine whilst staring at Simon, but two men in their twenties
introduced themselves in halting English as Jojo and Claude,
they were electricians and happy to provide him with quotes if

required.

The subject turned to the mill and the plans Simon had for it, and he sadly acknowledged that for the oldest part of the building he may need to employ specialist artisan workers, however, he was sure he could pass some work to local artisans when he reached that stage.

Henri's wife, Marie arrived breathless from the upstairs restaurant and began the necessary interrogation demanded of all new arrivals, and the other bar inhabitants stretched their ears to hear.

No, Madame Parker would not be joining him here; no, he had no children; yes, he intended on making St Honoré a permanent home; and no, he was definitely not a millionaire. Marie was crestfallen; there was hardly any gossip she could offer her regular customers and she returned upstairs to her diners.

After two beers, Philippe indicated he was leaving, and Simon paid the bar bill and followed him out.

'Beware those two rogues, Jojo and Claude – if you decide to use them ensure you have written *devis* first. But, their work is good and they know I am your friend now.' he said in a low voice as they walked back to the house.

'Who was the man with the Salvador Dali moustache?' Simon asked.

'Oh, that's Jacques. He *claims* he is an artist! He was annoyed that you bought the mill – he was waiting to buy it at a knock-down price, although he is - *en anglais* - poor as a church mouse; we say *gueux comme un rat d'église*. Also, he is your neighbour, and is not a pleasant fellow, so prepare for some bad feeling there.'

'My neighbour?'

'Yes, he owns that *rustique* shack downstream from you.' Philippe laughed.

They walked back through empty streets and past houses with the shutters all closed, the village getting ready to settle down for the night. An owl hooted nearby and Simon unsuccessfully scanned the rooftops, before his eyes widened at the clear sky and the myriad of bright stars. There were a lot worse places to live, he thought with a smile, trying to keep up with Philippe.

When they arrived at the house, Simon thanked his companion, and went to bed. It had been a long day, and he had much to think about, including the repetitive text messages from his soon-to-be ex-wife. The lumpy mattress fought back as he tried to get comfortable, and it was well after midnight when he finally fell asleep.

He woke with a start at seven, with the alarmingly loud ringing of the church bells. After his initial shock, he lay for a few minutes in the incredibly uncomfortable bed, listening to the villagers as they visited the *boulangerie*. After a few minutes with his ears ringing, he got up, stretched stiffly and dressed. He'd had better nights sleep in his car, he thought to himself as he made his way stiffly downstairs.

Madame Cholet presented him with a steaming bowl of hot chocolate and a plate of croissants and bread. He noted that she failed to inquire if he had slept well, and ate quickly before escaping into the cold sunshine. Today was a shopping day and he drove to Périgueux to a large DIY store to buy some supplies, and a new mailbox for the mill, before detouring on the return journey to Sarlat, to visit the architect he had employed.

***

Lunch was a *croque-monsieur*, eaten as he walked around the beautiful medieval centre, admiring the old architecture and square, whilst trying to avoid the many tourists. The architect's office was on the third floor of a medieval tower just off the main square, and he was thankfully efficient, having arranged for Simon to meet the main artisans for the renovation project, who would be arriving en-masse on the following Monday.

'I will be there initially,' he explained to Simon, 'to instil urgency. You must keep on at them or the two hour lunch will stretch and stretch.'

'I'll be there all the time myself,' Simon explained. 'I've rented a village room for a month, but want to be living on site as soon as possible. I've arranged for someone from the Federation of Mills to visit on Monday morning, so we can discuss anything then.'

After an hour discussing initial work schedules and priorities, Simon left with yet more paperwork. France seemed to be a country that loved bureaucracy and reams and reams of paper! As he walked back towards his car he also reflected that France also seemed to be full of people drinking coffee or a glass of wine and loving life. Perhaps one day I'll be sitting taking it easy, he mused as he virtuously denied temptation and strode to the car.

*****

The next few days were busy, and Simon finally managed to mow the meadow surrounding the mill and cleared most of the rubble from inside the mill building. With Philippe's help he secured an enormous skip which he filled before the weekend with the old timber, slates and accumulated rubbish from the mill buildings. At least he could now see the state of the buildings inside, and was generally pleased that he hadn't discovered the dreaded termites, although there was some woodworm damage, which could be simply and cheaply treated.

The electrician had visited and almost cried when he had seen the ancient and very unsafe supply. Simon explained that the adjoining cottage must be completed first as this would be his home for the foreseeable future, and the electrician sucked his teeth, and prepared a list which Simon then edited with a knowing frown before sending him off in his van to make the purchases. As an experienced builder, he had a fair idea of the requirements, and wasn't having the wool pulled over his eyes;

but building supplies in France were proving eye-watering, and he didn't need contractors trying to over engineer his simple requirements.

Chapter 2

As the temperatures rose, the water level of the stream feeding the mill pond dropped. He had two outlets, one from the mill pond, to feed the leat that powered the (for the moment) non-existent millwheel, and the other to divert the water downstream which would eventually empty into the Dordogne. For now both sluices were open just enough to keep the water moving, but he knew that before winter he'd have to remove the silt from under the remains of the wheel, and clear the overgrown willows and weed, or he'd have flooding issues.

Curious villagers had visited; either on the pretext of walking their dogs, or just for an evening *promenade*, and he was happy to stop and chat about the plans he had, and to hear their memories about the mill. His attempts to converse in French met polite smiles and corrections, but he was trying, and they seemed to appreciate it.

***

The *maire* arrived on Monday to join the architect and the contractors, and generously offered a delivery of *calcaire* for the driveway into the site, which the architect immediately accepted and indicated where this would be most beneficial, informing Simon that summer storms would turn the *chemin* into a quagmire.

Finally, that evening, he was alone, albeit surrounded by a mini-digger, and various pieces of equipment that the contractors left on site. The enormity of renovation, coupled with his abominably poor language skills was not insurmountable; but he wondered at the expectations of the villagers. They seemed pleased that he'd bought and was renovating the mill. He was waved to and smiled at around the village and was beginning to enjoy not just being a face amongst thousands that was so normal in the big cities in the UK. In his head at the start of this project he simply envisioned doing up the mill with the intention of living there until he'd decided how to move on with his life, but the whole project had acquired a life of its own and was in danger of running away with itself.

***

He walked back to his lodgings and stopped to pass the time of day with Émilie, who was tying up tiny tomato plants against the *boulangerie* wall. He leaned on the low stone wall and enjoyed watching her efficiently bend and tie the stems. Her dark hair was tied back with a yellow ribbon and her ponytail sat on her tanned neck. At her feet, generally getting in the way was the small, ludicrously scruffy fawn and brown dog he'd seen before sleeping at the door of the *boulangerie*. After the last plant was tied in, she stood and decided that as he *obviously* had nowhere else to be, she'd take the opportunity of finding out more about this new villager. She invited him to sit, and disappeared into the house for a moment, before returning with two cold bottles of beer.

The dog threw itself at his feet, belly-up, and Simon obliged by rubbing her belly.

'Eloise likes you,' Émilie snorted, taking a long drink from the bottle, and stifled a yawn, 'Sorry. I have to get up *very* early and I am fatigued.'

'When do you start?'

'I have to light the ovens at five and get the bread in not too long afterwards', she grimaced, 'it's not too bad most days, but getting up in winter is difficult.'

'You speak excellent English.'

'I lived in London for a few years, but it is good you are

here, so I can practise. There are few English in the village.'

Eloise moved so she could sit on Simon's foot, and he took the opportunity to scratch her head, whilst revealing a little more about himself.

'My wife kept the dog,' he volunteered. 'We split up a few months ago.' It was hard to talk about, even after a few months and he cringed as the words came out with bitterness.

'Ha!' Émilie laughed and nodded, 'You are fortunate! My husband took the money and left *me* the bills and the dog!'

It was his turn to smile, '*She* left me for the double-glazing salesman.'

Her pretty nose wrinkled as she struggled to understand, and he tried again, '*Le vendeur double vitrage.*'

Émilie clapped her hands to her mouth in mock horror, although Simon could see the dimples in her cheeks, and the laughter flashing in her eyes.

'I think you should not tell anyone this, or they will laugh,' she smiled. 'The commune has enough to talk about without putting more wood on the fire.'

He smiled back, and shoved Eloise off his foot. He thought he'd said enough too, for the time being.

'Thank you for the beer Émilie and *bonne soirée*.'

'*Bonne nuit*, Simon. And how is the bed of Madame Cholet?' she asked with a final cheeky grin as she picked up the empty bottles.

'Torture,' he laughed as he walked around the corner to his lodgings.

***

The next morning, after a quick breakfast, and another unsatisfactory shower he drove to Sarlat and bought a solar shower, which he installed outside the barn at the mill. At least he would be able to have a decent wash even if he couldn't have a decent sleep, he reasoned. The workmen were steadily removing the tiles from the roof and marking any rotten timbers, and whistled and cheered when he stripped naked to shower. With the mill so close to the centre of the village, he was trying to be both discreet and quick, and managed to have a thorough wash and dress in fresh clothes in a few minutes. As he congratulated himself, he noticed out of the corner of his eye that Jacques, his neighbour was staring at him from the road. Simon waved but Jacques turned abruptly and got into an ancient car, driving off in a cloud of blue smoke. Perhaps this was the unpleasantness that both the *notaire* and Philippe Cholet had warned him about. He sighed and realised that you can't please all the people all of the time, and turned his attention to the woodwork of the windows of the cottage.

***

Whilst Simon began to remove rotten windows and shutters, Jacques drove his little car towards St Cyprien, his foot flat on the accelerator and his hands gripping the wheel with white knuckles. With his *Gaulois* hanging from his lip, he cursed the Englishman. It was bad luck. In a few months the building would have probably been reduced in price; and if only some rich Americans had bought more of his paintings he'd have been able to buy the damn place. Now this upstart; this *stranger* would be able to delve into the secret recesses of the mill and discover where old man Renauld had hidden his gold.

He flicked the ash onto the filthy floor of the car and slowed down as he approached the Contrôl Technique centre, and parked outside. He'd have to make life difficult for the Englishman he decided and rolled the ends of his moustache, and that shouldn't be too hard to do. After all, he smiled, how hard could it be to arrange some little setbacks to force the man to give up and return to England?

***

The test would take an hour, the Inspector informed him, and Jacques walked across the road to the bar tabac for coffee, his mind full of anger. When he returned the car had failed and the Inspector was intent on showing him the faulty brakes pipes. With the car on the ramps, he pointed to the flexi-pipes, and explained that deterioration could result in a fatal failure of the brakes. All the pipes required replacing and must be done within two months to pass the test. Jacques was almost incandescent with rage and the Inspector shrugged, handing him the failure sheet.

Instead of returning home to finish the canvas of the beautiful woman he'd copied from a rival's website, he reluctantly drove to the local garage in the valley to arrange for the job to be done. Bernard wiped his hands on a rag and quoted a sum of a few hundred euros, echoing the concerns raised by the C.T. Inspector. Suddenly Jacques was listening intently, the seeds of an idea growing in his imagination, and he immediately arranged for the work to be done by the end of the week. He drove home smiling and laughing to himself, his bad mood gone; convinced that this information could be the very thing he needed to solve his little problem of the Englishman. After all; *accidents* happened all the time, he smiled lighting another cigarette.

Back at his small cottage he donned his painting smock and threw the front door open, flooding the dim and cramped room with natural light and some much needed fresh air. *Nude taking a bath* was on the easel, and Jacques worked quickly, stopping every so often to refresh his memory by examining the flimsy copy he'd printed from the computer. With some more masterpieces like this, the mill would soon be his. It was now just a little matter of arranging an accident, then waiting for the mill to be up for sale again. With a twirl of his moustache he smiled and lit another cigarette.

***

At the *boulangerie*, Émilie had finished cleaning down for the day. She pulled on her jeans and called Eloise for a walk and began to walk towards the mill pond. From her bakery she had caught glimpses and heard the noise from what was now a building site, but the men were at dinner now, and the noise had ceased for two hours. A couple of coots were swimming on the farthest side of the pond, darting in and out of the reeds, and swallows dipped and picked off some of the insects on the pond. Always inquisitive, Eloise bounded off into the bushes at the margins of the meadow, whilst Émilie noted with some pleasure the amount of work that Simon had accomplished in just a few days. The meadow had been cut and strimmed and the litter and debris removed, somehow enlarging the area hugely. A pile of broken and old roof tiles lay to one side of the main mill building and the bare roof was showing new replacement beams, ready for the new tiles to be fitted. The shadow of decay was lifting and the sun shone on the ochre stonework, hinting at the possibility of beauty waiting to be revealed. She walked back along the *chemin*, calling Eloise, who appeared from the bushes even more bedraggled than usual. In the passageway between the mill and the *boulangerie* she met Madame Cholet, carrying in her bags from a shopping trip.

'I saw you looking at the *moulin*,' she smiled. 'He's making progress, but it must be costing him.'

'Yes, I suppose,' Émilie agreed.

'He told Philippe he's going to reinstate the wheel.'

'Oh yes?'

'A miller and a baker would be a good match,' Madame Cholet whispered with a grin.

Émilie rolled her eyes with annoyance, '*He's* married. *I'm* married. And I don't think he'll ever be a miller!' she snorted, walking back into the cool sanctuary of her *boulangerie*.

Madame Cholet carried the bags inside her own house with a smile. She'd overheard them having a beer together the previous evening and they seemed to get on well. Of course it was perfectly friendly, perfectly respectable; but oh so deliciously interesting; and she was determined to see what direction the friendship was heading.

Philippe had arrived home from work, and was preparing the dinner tonight, and she handed him the pork steaks she'd bought. He'd already prepared the stuffing to make the *paupiettes,* and quickly rolled the thin steaks around the sausage, mushroom and herb stuffing, tying them up individually and placing them in a dish. He looked at her sideways and saw her smiling. Obviously she was dying to impart some gossip she had, and he rewarded her impatience with a tiny smile.

'What?'

'Simon Parker and Émilie Fournier.'

'Leave it alone woman. Can't a man speak to a woman without you imagining something?'

She kissed him on the cheek and laughed, taking a bottle of white wine from the fridge and placing it on the table. Philippe grunted, and placed a fresh baguette and a green salad on the table. Dinner would be forty minutes, so he'd have enough time to visit his neighbour to pass the time of day. He popped the wine back in the fridge, wiped his hands on a tea towel and walked round to the mill.

Simon was looking at the overgrown willow growing near the mill pond, and Philippe joined him.

'You need to remove it completely or the roots will find the water and breach the walls of the *étang,*' he said.

'Not just cut it down?'

'*Non*; its willow. It will just grow again. Dig around the base and then pull it out with the car.'

They stood quietly, thinking about this.

'I will come tomorrow and help you; after work.' Philippe offered.

Simon barely had time to thank him before Philippe turned and walked back to his house. He wasn't eating with the Cholet's tonight, but had decided to try one of the restaurants in nearby Les Eyzies, and changed into clean clothes before driving off.

***

The air was still warm and the sky still blue when he sat down at a table and chose from a small menu. Whilst he waited, he sipped a cold glass of white wine and watched as families and couples took their seats alongside him. The imposing rock faces of the cliffs with their myriad of caves towered above the town, and he was just beginning to relax when his mobile phone began to ring annoyingly. He looked at the number and inwardly groaned as he recognised the number.

'Jenn,' he answered curtly.

'Simon, you're a *nightmare* to get hold of!' she trilled down the phone. 'Harry said to ask why you're being so *difficult* about the settlement?' she wheedled.

He hated that voice she put on, and the fact that Harry; her solicitor was using her to get at him.

'I've already told you *and* Harry that my solicitor is dealing with the divorce and *not* to bother me Jenn. If you're going to persist in harassing me, I'll simply change my phone number. We're finished and I'm moving on, and frankly, you're lucky you're getting what I've agreed to, all things considered. Now go away, I'm going to eat.'

'Alone?' she asked archly just as he disconnected the call.

As his bread and main course arrived he wondered what he'd ever seen in her. Oh, she was gorgeous, but it had taken him sadly, too long to discover the selfishness, the childishness and the manipulation. Anyway, lesson learned; there'd be no more high maintenance, fickle, tantrum-throwing females in his life ever. He surveyed the dish of roast duck slices, separated with slivers of goats cheese, the fresh green salad and plate of tomatoes drizzled with truffle oil and picking up his knife and fork, immediately forgot about the soon-to-be ex-Mrs Parker.

***

Eventually, after putting a pillow at the bottom of the bed to allow his feet to hang over the footboard, Simon managed to fall asleep around about midnight. Madame Cholet's room was cheap, but he'd had enough of the too-short bed, lumpy mattress and dribbly shower, and he decided that he'd have to move into the mill cottage as soon as possible. It was either that or visit an osteopath for the increasing pain he had in his back and shoulders. The sun was beating down at eight when he walked down to the mill, relieved to see the workers already on-site and at least making noise, if not actively working.

Of the three main buildings on site the barn was the sorriest looking and unfit to camp out in. In the adjoining mill, although new beams and timbers filled the roof void, it would be weeks before the roof would be in place and then they'd have to start ripping out the damaged floor. He couldn't sleep there. The tiny shed where he had locked his tools away had no electricity yet and was dark and dank. Finally, he looked at the small cottage attached to the mill. Whilst it wasn't welcoming, it was watertight and free from damp. He called the electrician over and pleaded with him to install some sort of basic supply, a couple of sockets and a light fitting to help him move in. Finally, after the promise of an envelope stuffed with cash, the electrician promised he'd sort something makeshift by the next day.

Simon kept a beady eye on him, and was pleased to see him rigging up some cabling and sockets, whilst he helped the artisans by removing the rubbish to the skip and clearing their working area. Inside the upper floor of the cottage, a look upwards revealed daylight peeping through in a few areas, so Simon clambered up the scaffolding to remove the broken or cracked tiles and replace them with good ones salvaged from the mill roof. Insulation boards were cut and fitted inside the roof void and the hours flew by. Suddenly the workers were shouting to him that they were going home.

He looked at his watch and groaned to see it was after six. He returned to the front of the cottage, and listened to the electrician who confirmed he'd have a decent supply in the cottage in the next day or two. Progress of some sort, he thought as he watched Philippe drive in with a tractor. Of course; the willow, he remembered.

They shook hands and began the job of chainsawing the willow into a substantial stump and then digging around the trunk to loosen it. A heavy chain was slung round the trunk and secured, and Philippe got back in the tractor and began to pull the tree out.

It was almost dark when they finally finished, and with a grunt, Philippe shook his hand and drove away to get his dinner.

Simon headed to the *Salamandre* for a pizza and a beer and sat eating with just Henri for company, before heading back to his lodgings. He informed Madame Cholet that he would only need the room for the next week, and offered to take them out to the restaurant in Les Eyzies on his final night as a thank-you. Madame was enchanted and accepted happily, and Simon climbed the stair to his room. As the small bed creaked alarmingly with his weight, he told himself that in a week, he'd be able to sleep in a proper bed, and maybe even have a lie-in without the sound of bells ringing in his head in the mornings. He drifted off quickly, half dreaming of luxurious mattresses, and power showers. Soon, he murmured to himself, soon.

Chapter 3

The clanging of the bells woke him at seven, and he rose and stretched tiredly. Six more nights, he told himself with a groan. It was beginning to feel like Groundhog Day… He scowled at the old shower and turned his back on it, pulling his working clothes on and walked stiffly down the stairs. Hot chocolate and *pains au chocolat* put him in a better mood and he walked outside into the sunshine and round to the mill. The tree they had hauled out the previous evening needed cut up and moved away, and he unlocked the shed door and got out his chainsaw and protective clothing. He'd tackle this now, before the heat made it too uncomfortable, and soon the peace and quiet in the tiny village was ruined, as he took the limbs from the trunk and then sliced the trunk into sections. He watched as the workers arrived and continued to re-roof the mill building, the plumbers noisily feeding pipes and cabling through the thick stone walls. Everyone was busy and the time flew quickly as the temperatures climbed. At lunch-time, he made himself a makeshift baguette of cheese and ham, as the others headed to the *Salamandre* for their lunch.

Removing the fallen tree to the margin of the meadow took all day, and at six, as he sat alone outside the mill doorway and drunk from a bottle of beer, he was pleased to see that removing the tree had allowed a vast amount of sunlight around the buildings. The tree had been unlucky; growing in the wrong place and Simon decided that once the buildings had been renovated, he would plant replacements in more suitable areas of the land.

The stones of the mill and cottage absorbed the heat of the sun and on entering the cottage he was pleased at the transformation so far. Soon he would have a proper bedroom. Tomorrow he'd collect his bed and mattress from the storage unit he was renting near Sarlat, and reassemble it in the cottage, but for the next few nights Madame Cholet's little bed with its grid-iron mattress and confining footboard were what he had to look forward to every evening.

He sat in the evening sun outside the cottage door watching the dragonflies darting over the surface of the diminishing *étang*, and drowsed. His eyelids drooped and Simon closed his eyes for a few moments, enjoying the tranquillity and the warmth. A cuckoo was calling distantly from the woods as he relaxed, and then the serenity of the moment was ruined by a loud splash.

Simon's eyes snapped open to see Eloise in the *étang*, paddling furiously after a duck. He watched the silly dog, which hadn't a hope of catching the duck, and became aware of Émilie calling her name repeatedly. The duck disappeared with the stream leading out of the pond, leaving Eloise floundering in the muddy shallows.

Philippe and his wife had appeared from their house to see what the commotion was, and at the far side of the *étang*, Jacques also appeared from his cottage to view the spectacle.

It suddenly occurred to Simon that the dog was struggling to free herself from the deep silty bottom of the pond. The same thing obviously had occurred to Émilie, who marched to the pond, hitched her skirt around her waist and waded in.

As she slowly waded towards the dog, Philippe and Madame Cholet joined Simon, and Jacques sat on the opposite bank and lit a cigarette, watching the spectacle with some amusement.

Grabbing the dog by the scruff of the neck, Émilie pulled and rocked the dog free, and dragged her back to the bank, covering herself with mud in the process. She was furiously cursing and shouting at the beast, under the rapt attention of the audience.

Simon ran to help her out of the *étang* and she hauled the mud-soaked dog out onto the bank beside her. Philippe and his wife automatically stepped back, lest the dog shook the mud free, scattering the audience with souvenirs of the incident, whilst Simon offered her the use of the solar shower and towels.

Philippe and his wife clucked around her whilst she held the dog under the warm water to remove most of the offending mud.

'Mon Dieu, l'odeur!' she cried, '*Un bain est nécessaire immédiatement*!' Simon wondered if she was referring to the dog or herself, and decided that a tactful silence was the best response. She then rinsed the mud from her own bare legs, before snatching the towel to dry herself and allow her skirt to cover her legs once more. Then slipping her sandals back on, she angrily called the dog to heel and marched around the corner to her home, with Madame Cholet followed her to help; leaving Philippe and Simon standing uselessly.

Across the pond, with the event now over, Jacques stirred himself, and with a twirl of his moustache exclaimed, 'Magnificent legs! She should model for one of my paintings!' as he pressed his fingers to his lips with a kiss, and turned to return to his home.

Philippe lingered a few minutes, looking at the progress the builders had made then reluctantly said his goodnight to Simon. 'I will return and see if all is calm and the dog is safe,' he said with a smile, 'and Jacques is correct for once; she does have *magnificent* legs.'

He shook Simon's hand and walked back to his house, leaving Simon to lock up. As he lay that evening in the bed of torture, his mind kept going back to the sight of her with her skirt hitched up and her long tanned legs being washed under the shower. He pulled one thin pillow from behind his head and buried his head under it crossly. It was bad enough trying to sleep in this awful bed, but trying to sleep with his mind on Émilie Fournier's legs wasn't helping at all!

***

The next morning at the *boulangerie*, Émilie was busy putting baguettes and *pains de campagne* in the baskets ready to sell, with an unhappy Eloise now chained to the outside table in the garden of the *boulangerie*. Simon arrived at seven and bought some baguettes, some goat's cheese and a bottle of Perrier to take with him to the mill, and enquired if all was well this morning. She blushed prettily, but explained that Eloise was now incarcerated to prevent any more mischief. Simon took the opportunity to reassure her that once the water level in the *étang* dropped a little more he would ensure that the both it and the old wheel pit would be dredged of the silt and that the summer storms would soon fill the pond back to a high level in case Eloise wished a little swim in cleaner water. This obviously didn't go down too well, and the fastidious young woman wrinkled her nose. He decided that perhaps it was time to go, and as he turned his back to leave, she stopped him.

'What are you going to do with the silt?' she asked, 'It would be good to have a little for the garden here; unless you are going to begin a little *potager* of your own? Some potimaron and butternut squash would enjoy the rich soil and the high water level.'

'I'm really a bit busy with the building work, and I don't know much about growing fruit or veg,' he admitted. 'In fact, I don't really know much about plants at all; unless you want to educate me.'

She stared at him, unsure if he was just attempting to be friendly, or if he really wanted her help. With her tiny garden outside the *boulangerie*, she yearned to plant some fruit trees, but didn't have the space. But the lure of organising a proper garden was irresistible.

'We could chat about the land this evening, if you are free?' he suggested. 'Come over and I'll show you what I think, and you could suggest some plants or trees or things,' he finished

31

lamely. 'I'm sorry, I'm not a gardener.'

'Perhaps,' she replied noncommittally, turning to serve an old lady who was waiting to buy bread.

***

Feeling as if he'd been dismissed, he left with his food and walked down to the mill, putting the food into a bag in the cottage and then hitching his car to his trailer, drove to Sarlat to collect his bed. What was he *thinking*, he asked himself as he drove. He'd basically just asked her out, and that wasn't his intention. He really did need some help with the landscaping, and France being so much warmer from the UK, he was unsure what to plant. He'd admired the peach and plum trees in the village and envied the villagers with their pristine little *potager's*, but that was a whole new world to him.

In Bristol, his apartment didn't have a private garden, and his dad's house just had a small lawn. Now he owned three acres of meadow and woodland, and was more than a little out of his depth. He needed help; that was obvious, but didn't want his new neighbours to think he was trying to romance the baker, even if the idea was starting to appeal to him despite his better judgement.

Sarlat was busy. Wednesday was market day and he wandered around buying cheese, olives, some salad and big, beefy tomatoes. He succumbed to the temptation of popping into a wine shop and bought two bottles of a very nice pecharmant wine and then forced himself to return to the car. A short drive and he arrived at his storage unit, and with a little imagination managed to load his dismantled bed into the trailer. It was getting warm and the perspiration beaded on his forehead as he finally closed the trailer ramp, secured it and began the twenty minute drive home. Home. Was it *really* home yet?

He mulled the question over as he drove. He certainly hadn't thought much about Bristol or the UK, hadn't watched any TV, let alone British TV since arriving, and was beginning to settle into rural life. He was glad to be free of his cheating wife, and his father had phoned him only once to check up on him, relating that the weather was the same, if not worse; that the state of the country was the same, if not worse and asked when he'd be visiting. Simon recalled being evasive. It was early days, he was busy, and he'd be in touch. The memory hurt. Dad was in his eighties, and alone. As an only child, Simon felt the twin shadows of responsibility and guilt at not being there and decided that he must make a flying visit soon to see him. The urgency to make a home for himself at the mill heightened, and he pulled over to the side of the road and called the architect asking for an on-site meeting next week to review progress. This done, he rolled the windows down, put on the radio and forced himself to listen to the banal euro-pop music from France Bleu Perigord for the remainder of the journey back to the old mill.

***

He unloaded the bed and was about to carry the frame into the cottage, then stopped. Inside was a thick layer of dust, so he grabbed a brush and swept it all out, before taking a few minutes to let the haze settle and then reassembling the bed inside the main living area. Jojo had installed a few sockets and a light bulb hung from the centre of the room, and Simon smiled. So, it was a bit basic, but not that much different from the room he was renting at the Cholet's. At least the bed was the right size and the mattress comfortable. He could slum it for a few weeks until the builders finished the plastering.

Today Monsieur Durand the chimney sweep was arriving to inspect and clean the chimneys of the cottage and the mill. Simon knew that work would be required before installing liners for wood-burners, and the new wood-burners themselves, but everything had to be done a step at a time, and he had to curb his impatience.

He ate his picnic lunch and decided to take the afternoon off.

A watched pot never boils he told himself and walked to the *Salamandre* where the builders were enjoying their long lunch. He explained to Claude that he'd be back late in the afternoon, to supervise the others and to explain to Mr Durand what was required, and then; refusing the proffered small, strong coffee, returned to his car. This afternoon, he was visiting Castelnaud-la-Chapelle and being a tourist for a few hours.

***

He parked in the top car park and walked down into the village. Traditional ochre stone houses surrounded the château on three sides and tumbled down the steep hill to the river below. Today, he would explore the village itself, but leave the château for another day. There were many cafes, bistros and more than a few tourist shops. Medieval was the theme with children's toys like wooden swords and hobby-horses, shields and heraldic decoration, and in one shop, he found a couple of beautiful blacksmith-made table lamp stands, which he thought would look perfect inside the cottage. He paid for them, and told the shop-keeper he'd collect them in half an hour on his way back up the hill, and she delightedly set them aside for him.

The narrow cobbled streets wound down to the bottom of the hill and he found himself facing the river and a well-located bar and restaurant. Taking a seat under a parasol, he ordered a beer and sat people watching, whilst he rested.

A family at the next table had two perfectly behaved young children, and he sat and watched them interact. Some friends arrived with their own slightly older children, and the parents exchanged *bisous*, the traditional kisses of greeting, whilst the children disappeared towards the river. The canoe hire was busy, as the schools were closed on Wednesday afternoons, and the far-off laughter and chatter from the river was pleasant to listen to. Unused to leisure-time, Simon fidgeted and finally finished his beer and began to climb back up into the village, collected his purchases and returned to the car, hot and sweaty.

When he returned to the mill, Claude informed him that Mr Durand had swept the chimneys, and handed Simon the *facture* or bill, 'The old fox wanted to charge you more, but I insisted he charge you the normal rate we pay,' he grinned, clapping Simon on the back, 'You owe me a *pastis*,' he said returning to the mill house and the wiring. Simon saw that they had indeed been busy, with the electrical wiring snaking through discreet holes in the stonework. Jojo explained that the walls were more than half a metre thick and getting the holes drilled had been a stop and start job to save the life of the drills, but the network of wiring was now finished in both the mill and the cottage and they had to await connection from the electricity company now.

The heat increased towards the end of the afternoon and work inevitably slowed down. The air was thick and humid and large clouds were building-up in the western sky.

They stopped work at six and the men washed using the solar shower they had previously scorned, before heading to the *Salamandre* for a drink before returning home. They insisted Simon join them, with Jojo explaining with a grin and wiggling his eyebrows, that *cinq à sept* was an old French tradition. Between the hours of five and seven in the evening used to be the time to meet one's mistress before going home to the wife and family. Nowadays, they would settle for an *aperitif* before going home. They sat outside the bar and admired the *moulin* across the road.

'The building is responding to us now', Claude said philosophically.

When Simon threw him a questioning look he explained.

'Now all the vegetation has been cleared, the stones are breathing again. The dampness is retreating and the timbers inside the building look healthier. This makes the work easier for us.'

Jojo nodded in agreement, 'But we are to have a storm in the next day or so, so be vigilant,' he wagged a finger, and downed his *pastis*. 'See you tomorrow,' he said and disappeared to his car.

After ordering and eating a pizza, Simon made his way back into the centre of the village and as he passed the *boulangerie*, Émilie leaned out from the upstairs window calling, 'Coucou!'

He looked up and smiled.

'If you are free now, I will come to the mill to see the land and give you some ideas.'

He waited till she ran downstairs, shut Eloise firmly inside the house and appeared holding a pad of paper and a pen. They walked back around the corner and stood at the entrance to the mill.

She explained that because the mill was naturally low lying there would be a high water level in the soil at most times of the year, which made sense to him. The higher, wooded land would provide him with some firewood; she would give him the name of the man who would come and cut some of the older trees for him in December, but this year he would need to order around six *stéres* of firewood; again she would give him the contact details.

The meadow if fenced properly would be able to support a small flock of sheep she began, and Simon shook his head.

'I'm no farmer', he said, 'I like the idea, but don't want the responsibility.'

'I will speak to Jojo; he has sheep that can stay on the meadow for the summer at least. In high summer, his land dries out and has no grass, so he will be glad. You can make an arrangement that he has one lamb butchered for you in exchange.'

This was an excellent idea, Simon concurred, and Émilie told him she would tell Jojo to organise and pay for the fencing also, 'It is only fair.'

He was impressed. In the space of ten minutes, she had come up with two marvellous ideas to utilise the majority of his land. He indicated the area around the mill and cottage, 'I need a large parking area here, but it needs to be pretty and easy to maintain,' he said.

'You need a nice tree for shade just outside the cottage, then you can eat or entertain outside,' she suggested and wrote something on the pad. 'And if you have some stone walls here around the house, you could also plant some fruit trees.'

'I'd prefer them to be over there, beside the *étang*', he said. 'Then it could be a small orchard and I could have a few ducks...'

Émilie smiled, 'Ducks are messy. They will make the *étang* muddy and they *squirt*. If you really want them, put their house beside the stream on the low side of the *étang*, then the water will wash away the mud and poop.'

He nodded in agreement, pleased at the sensible suggestion.

'The rest can wait until you have finished building,' Émilie smiled, and they walked back together, saying goodnight at the corner. Her enthusiasm had put a little colour in her cheeks and she had been twittering excitedly at the plans for the land.

'I will look at some fruit trees for your *verger* and give you a list,' she said as she opened her door, trying to keep naughty Eloise from escaping.

'Thank you,' Simon said smiling, 'That's been really useful. Goodnight.'

In an instant it seemed that they were both reluctant to call it an evening and a frisson of something ethereal but almost tangible seemed to touch them both. She smiled and dropped her gaze, slipping inside her house quickly, leaving him there; wondering.

***

In the bedroom of horrors it was so humid it was like moving through treacle. He threw open the bedroom window, and then realised it would make no difference. The air was thick and heavy and he pulled off his tee shirt and threw it in a corner. As night fell, he folded up the duvet and placed it on the chair in his room, content to sleep without a covering, and lay on the short bed with his feet sticking out the sides. Honestly, did she normally rent the room to *dwarves*? he wondered crossly. At six foot Simon wasn't overly tall, but the footboard prevented him even allowing his feet to overhand, and the mattress was so old and thin he could feel the iron springs poking into his skin every few inches. Around midnight the rain broke with large, fat raindrops bouncing off the shutters. As the clouds released their heavy load of water, the thundering shower woke him in time to close the window against the deluge. At least the temperature had dropped, and he slept a little better afterwards, pulling the duvet back onto the bed, with a fleeting wish that someone with long tanned legs would be ideal to snuggle up to.

Chapter 4

The next morning it continued to rain heavily. Work on the mill and the buildings moved inside now that the roof had been covered with new tiles, and the men happily worked securing the new beams for the upper level floor in the mill. Ladders sufficed at the moment as the stair the architect had ordered was still being manufactured, and by lunchtime a criss-cross network of beams was more or less complete. The workmen moved across the remaining lattice like rats, with cables strung like Christmas lights fastened loosely until the floorboards could be fitted.

Philippe arrived at the end of lunchtime to show Simon how to control the rising flow of water at the *vannes* or sluices controlling the leats. Water pooled in depressions in the calcaire-covered yard, and they picked their way towards the *étang*.

'You must keep watch on the weather. If the leat floods you will have a quagmire in the land and possibly inside the buildings,' he warned, handing the large metal key back to Simon. The mill pond level had risen quickly and the water, previously clear was now muddy. Simon was suddenly aware of how precarious living at a watermill might be if you didn't keep an eye on weather forecasts.

He made a mental note to clear the margins of the exiting stream as soon as the weather improved and the rain stopped, but meanwhile, there was nothing he could do, and so he scanned the dark sky and prayed for the rain to stop, placing the key at the entrance of the tool shed in case he needed to find it quickly.

Philippe clapped his back, 'Relax! It's just a new way of life for you now. You will get accustomed to it.'

He left and Simon returned to the task of installing the new wooden windows in the mill cottage, taking advantage of the break in the rain, as the yard outside the mill cottage steamed in the warmth. By the end of the afternoon, three windows had been installed before the next opening of the heavens, and Simon was pleased at the amount of light now flooding the cottage. Progress was slow, but rewarding and the cottage was taking shape.

He sat that evening at the *Salamandre*, eating his pizza and salad pleased at how everything was coming together. The next morning his oak floorboards for the upper level of the mill were being delivered, which he estimated would take a couple of days to fit. He finished his glass of red wine off and bid goodnight to Henri and Marie, and even Jacques; who was sitting in his usual corner, scowling bitterly at Simon. Back at the Cholet's he undressed slowly and went to bed. The rain slapped his window wetly, and Simon slept uneasily, half-listening and hoping the rain would stop sometime soon.

***

Jacques turned his collar up and walked past the *moulin* towards his own cottage. He sneered at the progress, and delighting in the rain which would hamper the Englishman in his work. He'd been dismayed at how quickly Simon Parker had cleared the vegetation, and begun the huge task of renovation. At the rate he was going he would soon be working on the lower floor of the mill and was bound to discover the old miller's secret stash of gold, which Jacques believed was hidden somewhere in the mill. The *meteo* forecast was stating that the rain would stop the next afternoon, which infuriated him. He wanted the rain to continue, to slow the builder down, but over the weather he had no control, he scowled; shaking his fist at the sky. As he plodded back to his house an evil idea began to form in his mind. He'd seen Philippe showing Simon how to control the flow of water in the *vannes*. He'd seen them place the key beside the tool shed. Wouldn't it be a shame if clever Simon Parker forgot to open the *vanne* downstream on the leat leaving his property? It was located in the overgrown vegetation at the edge of Jacques own property. Water had to find its own level and if it overflowed from the small stream then the only place for it to go would be the yard surrounding the buildings, perhaps even *into* the buildings! That would *surely* hamper the Englishman. If the rain continued through the night, it might *even* cause some damage; he thought gleefully and twirled his moustache. He decided to give the water a helping hand and open the *vanne* on the *étang* also, releasing the rising water from the millpond. Back at his house, Jacques excitedly searched for a flashlight, picked up his own *vanne* key and then, after midnight crept outside and along the boundary towards the mill. He could hear the stream rushing along beside him and simply followed the noise until he reached the first *vanne*. Mr Parker made it *too* easy – the grass had been strimmed and Jacques had no difficulty in quietly slipping the key on the sluice and lowering it into the water. When it reached the bottom, he followed the stream to the outlet on the millpond.

He was close to the houses now and despite the hour and the weather, he needed to be careful. With his heart hammering in his chest he inserted the key. It squeaked crossly, and he gave it a couple of turns, listening in the dark to the satisfying whoosh of water escaping before furtively back-tracking to his own land. Back in his own dank cottage he poured a celebratory glass of *eau de vie* and turned in for the night, listening delightedly to the heavy rain.

***

At seven Simon was awakened by a loud banging downstairs. Émilie Fournier was hammering on the front door and calling loudly for the Cholets. Simon got up and dressed quickly, almost running downstairs. What on *earth* was happening? Philippe was pulling on a jacket and threw him a spare,

'Quickly! There is a flood!'

Accompanied by Émilie, who was talking non-stop, they ran to the mill. Simon's heart sank as he took in the flat expanse of muddy water lapping at the foundations of the building, where yesterday there was just a gravel yard. He was horrified and perplexed. *How* could this have happened? Yesterday he and Philippe had opened the *vanne* to prevent this very thing happening!

Philippe was angry. 'Quickly! The key!' he cried and strode to the *vanne* mounted on the *étang* exit point. Together, they fitted the key and slowly, against the pressure of the water they lowered the steel sluice, preventing any more water feeding into the flooded leat. Then Philippe turned to him, 'You must open the *vanne* downstream now. Open it *wide*, and be careful! You will need to wade through the water.'

Simon handed him his mobile phone and armed with the key, waded through the muddy water towards where he thought the leat was. The water became deeper, and was still moving, pulling at his legs and now soaking up his jeans to the knees.

'Be careful! Slowly!' Philippe called from the road. A couple of villagers had gathered at the roadside despite the downpour to see what the commotion was and looked horrified.

Simon edged forward, feeling the ground gingerly with outstretched feet and saw the top of the leat *vanne* mechanism just clear of the water in the overgrown meadow. He moved towards it and fitted the key. The pressure of the water against the metal sluice gate was immense, but he slowly wound it upwards, releasing the water downstream with a rush.

The rain was still hammering down, and he returned to the others, who had now been joined by Jojo, Claude and another of the workers.

'We will talk at home,' Philippe hissed. 'Send them home,

there is nothing to be done today.'

'But there's a *delivery* due!' Simon began.

Philippe turned to him angrily, 'And *how* are they going to deliver it? You must put them off till at least tomorrow, better the day after.'

He handed Simon his phone, 'Call them now.'

Philippe rapidly spoke to the awaiting workforce who shook their heads and dispersed. Émilie also returned to the *boulangerie* leaving the two men standing in the rain. 'Come; we talk inside,' Philippe said, marching back home, holding his jacket against the rain.

Madame Cholet had hot chocolate and glasses of brandy waiting for them, and, as they shrugged off their wet jackets, Émilie pushed the door open and sat down too.

Philippe downed the brandy in one and turned to Simon.

'Sabotage', he hissed. 'You and I ensured the *vanne* was opened half-way yesterday. You locked the key away – I *saw* you. This was deliberate.'

Simon finally managed to get hold of the wood yard on the 'phone and tried to delay the delivery in his halting French, until Philippe took the phone from him. In rapid French he explained the situation and then handed the phone back, 'They will come in two days. The water should have receded by then.'

'It could only be Jacques,' Philippe growled angrily. 'But we cannot *prove* it. You *must* start to sleep at the mill, and you need a guard dog!'

'Well, I can't live there yet!' Simon said, equally angrily. 'We need to wait until the water level drops and then I'll need to see how much has gone into the buildings.'

He couldn't believe that someone would stoop so low.

'We must call the *gendarmes*,' Philippe said grimly. 'If for no other reason than to make it clear that this will be taken seriously. I doubt that your insurance will pay anything as the buildings are not habitable.'

Émilie made her excuses – she had to deal with customers at

the *boulangerie*, and with a sad squeeze of Simon's shoulder left.

The *maire* arrived, having heard of the incident and sympathised with Simon. Philippe translated for him and the maire shrugged his shoulders, without proof there was nothing he could do, he explained.

The *gendarmes* arrived and took a report, but again, without proof, this was just a formality, they explained. Simon was furious, but helpless. They had to wait for the floodwater to recede before he could even see what damage, if any, had been done, and after changing into dry clothes, he gloomily returned periodically through the morning to the mill, willing the water to recede and praying for the rain to stop. At lunchtime, the clouds had emptied and blue sky and warmth returned, and everyone breathed a sigh of relief.

Émilie closed the *boulangerie* and took him lunch in a basket to where he stood at the top of the *chemin*, and he devoured the quiche and potato salad hungrily, as she watched.

By four pm, the water level had dropped somewhat, leaving a thick muddy deposit covering the yard. Simon walked around the buildings. The new tool shed door had a tide-mark about six inches from the ground and the water had penetrated within. He threw the door open and allowed the sunshine to begin the process of drying out. The yard began to steam and the smell of the mud drying was like decaying vegetation.

Mercifully, the cottage had been spared, with the water just reaching to the step outside, but not overflowing within. The mill, located slightly lower on the land *had* been breached and inside the floor was wet, but with no sign of water lying, and the stone walls and floor just needed the mud to dry-out before being brushed out and cleaned.

The leat was now almost back in its bed with a few puddles lying in the yard and around the low-lying meadow. A slight movement downstream drew Simon's eye. Jacques was standing watching, and when he saw Simon quickly hid himself from sight. Smothering his fury, Simon walked to the

Salamandre, deciding how to deal with the situation he faced. He was an interloper, not a local; and mustn't escalate the situation. There was no choice but for him to start sleeping in the cottage from now on, Marie and Henri advised as he ate his dinner. Jacques was nowhere to be seen, Simon was pleased to note. He didn't know if he could be trusted to sit in the same room as him with him being the prime suspect.

Jojo and Claude arrived, explaining they would be at work in the morning, even if it was just to clear mud and salvage what they could. This cheered Simon considerably; maybe the village was sympathising with him on what had been his lowest day since arriving. They all drank far too much and it was near midnight when Henri sent them home. He shook Simon's hand warmly, 'We are glad you chose St. Honoré as your home, do not let one person put you off. The village is happy for you to be here.'

Simon trudged back tiredly to the Cholet's. The house was in darkness and he let himself in and went to bed exhausted.

The next morning he dressed and drank hot chocolate with Madame Cholet. Émilie popped her head round the door and with a sweet smile, pressed some almond-paste croissants towards him, before disappearing as fast as she had appeared. His host chuckled and clucked and refilled his cup with more hot chocolate.

Perhaps the excess alcohol the previous night had done him some good, he mused. He'd slept fitfully and awoke determined and rested. The sun was streaming in through the open kitchen door and Simon ate as fast as he could; keen to start clearing up after the flooding at the mill. But when he rounded the corner he was amazed to see a whole army of people on-site. Claude caught him at the slope going down to the yard and shook his hand warmly, 'The village has come to help. The women are sweeping out the mud and cleaning, the men are re-laying some *calcaire* that the *maire* has provided.'

Émilie was directing the ladies, who were swilling out the

stone floor of the mill and the cottage. She waved and smiled to him, and for a second, Simon was caught unawares. His heart raced for a few seconds, brimming over as he realised that the villagers had gone out of their way to show him he'd been accepted. And especially that Émilie too seemed delighted to help. He clapped Claude on the back and followed him down into the yard. Jojo was pushing the machinery into the yard from the shed, checking it was undamaged and allowing it to air in the sunshine. Philippe was with a couple of the commune workers, at the leat, ensuring that the stream drained cleanly away from the mill and that another flooding "accident" couldn't possibly occur again.

Émilie came to talk to him, to introduce the older ladies of the village, who had given up their morning to help him. He smiled and thanked them warmly, and they giggled like schoolgirls at being singled-out.

At eleven the *maire* sounded his car horn from the road, and the villagers stopped. He announced that the *Salamandre* was providing food and the *mairie* providing the wine for lunch in the *salle de fetes* at twelve, with everyone who had helped invited. A great cheer went up and the villagers spent the next forty minutes finishing off the cleaning and generally tidying the mess that the floodwater had caused.

Lunch was a jolly and noisy affair, with Henri and Marie passing round bowls of rice, platters with roasted chicken thighs and bowls of dressed green salad. Bowls of olives slick with olive oil and platters of fresh bread from Émilie's *boulangerie* completed the meal. The *maire* walked round placing two bottles of rosé wine on each table. They laughed, talked and ate; and Simon had to stop and start every time a villager came forward to introduce themselves. At the end of lunch, he was introduced to some English residents too, Barrie and Sue, retirees who lived at the edge of the village; Brigitte, a Dutch artist who had lived in the village for twenty years and Didier, who helped in the *Salamandre* during the summer. Eventually, everyone began to drift off home, leaving Simon sitting with Émilie, Henri and Marie. They left the dishes and walked over to the mill. The water had now gone and the leat was back in its bed, looking innocent and playful, and the pond, although fuller, was benign and still.

'I have one more surprise' Émilie smiled and pointed to a trio of white geese.

'These will alert you to anyone coming into your land now', she laughed, 'And God help that snake Jacques if he wants to tackle them.'

The geese were patrolling the area noisily around the leat and water meadow, and Simon roared with laughter. Marie tactfully pulled Henri back to the bar with the reminder of washing-up and the two young people were left alone to sit on the wall overlooking the *étang*.

'Thank you,' he said quietly to her. 'That was very kind, and entirely unexpected.'

She wrinkled her nose again, 'The village is *very* cross at what he did. Oh yes, they *all* suspect Jacques, and the *maire* has visited him this morning too. That should be an end to it. We want to see the *moulin* back in order, and we all want you to stay Simon.'

She blushed prettily, and then jumped off the wall, 'Now, I have to clean and work, so, no more adventures today please.' And with a cheeky smile, she strode off in the direction of the *boulangerie*, leaving Simon to his mill.

He sat quietly for a few moments and then walked down the sloping *chemin*, now covered with new *calcaire* and into the yard, which was steaming in the sun. The doors of the mill were open and the floors washed and clean, the stone floor almost gleaming. There was no sign that the water had done any internal damage, he was relieved to see, and in the cottage, his bed was safe and dry, with a small old-fashioned table under the new window with a jug of wild flowers in it; a gift from one of the village matrons. Outside, the machinery was dry and he began to move it back into the tool shed. He'd know in a day or two whether the new shed door would warp with the moisture, but right now, everything looked fine. Just as the tension drained out of him the geese began to shriek and honk and he turned his head to see a flurry of movement at the boundary of his land and Jacques, spying covertly from the bushes. A secret smile played on his lips as he imagined the large birds getting hold of that silly Salavor Dali moustache and giving it a good tweak, and then he deliberately dismissed the sour old fool from his mind. The world was full of bitter people and he was determined not to be one of them. Today had proved to be a better day and he'd end it by driving to the *pépinière* that Émilie had suggested and see what fruit trees he could buy. With the windows wound down, and the radio on, he took the road to Montignac feeling buoyant and happy.

Chapter 5

The *pépinière* proved to be a large, family-run plant nursery, and thankfully; the son of the owner spoke excellent English. He took the list from Simon that Émilie had written and beckoned Simon outside to the area housing the fruit trees.

Together they chose two apples, two cherries, a pear that was already fan-trained and a Mirabelle plum. The nurseryman helped him squeeze the trees into the pick-up and shook Simon's hand, inviting him to return when he had decided on what plants he required for the rest of the garden.

Reluctant to return immediately, Simon turned off the road and visited the pretty village of Saint Leon sur Vezere. He parked in the shade, leaving the windows open a touch so the trees didn't fry in the mobile oven he was driving, and wandered to the river, watching canoes drifting downstream past the chateau and under the bridge before sitting at a table at the riverside café and enjoying a coffee. He pulled his phone out to capture the idyllic scene on the camera, and to his annoyance noted the six missed calls from his estranged wife. Well, Jenn was certainly persistent, he thought, and wondered if he should write Eddie a note of thanks for taking her off his hands. He popped the phone back in his pocket and finished his coffee, before driving slowly back through the Vezere Valley and arrived at Saint Honoré just before six.

***

Carefully unloading his trees he became aware of raised voices and looked up to see a very cross Émilie pointing an overdressed skinny blonde towards him. His heart sank as he recognised his wife, who screeched loudly as she attempted to walk down the *chemin* in very high heels, 'Simon darling! You *are* naughty; I've been trying to reach you since *yesterday*!'

'What are you doing here Jenn?' he asked quietly, aware that his neighbour was standing watching him with arms akimbo and a scowl on her face. Jenn Parker loudly air-kissed around his face and ignored the cool reception.

'So, *this* is your new gaff?' she sneered, taking in the building works. 'My God, *rustic* isn't the word! What were you *thinking* darling?'

Simon pushed her back slightly. Dressed in a short red sundress with totally unsuitable heels she looked very out of place in the small rustic village. In the months since she'd left him for the charms (and money) of Eddie the slick double-glazing man she still measured everything by her own dubious standards. Had she *actually* come all this way just to argue with him for a bigger settlement? The thought was distasteful, but sadly not inconceivable.

'Why are you here?'

'Well, Eddie and I are here for a long weekend; not *here*, you understand; we're staying in a nice hotel in Sarlat. So, I thought I'd come and see your new project *and* we could chat about you increasing my share in the divorce settlement,' she smiled, hooking her arm in his and trying to steer him towards the chemin and the *Salamandre*. 'Look, there's a little bar, let's have a glass of wine and talk.'

Simon braced himself and removed her arm, 'Jenn, I've told you before, the settlement is the settlement. I'm not increasing it and I'm *not* discussing this any more.'

'But darling!' she wailed, 'I can't be expected to slum it in Bristol. I can only just afford a *tiny* flat on what you offered; nothing for clothes or bills. I thought you loved me?' she finished with a trembling lip.

Simon had experienced her wheedling and whining before

and determinedly turned her towards the chemin, 'I thought so too Jenn, but these months without you have been bliss actually, and I'm not sure it was love I felt for you; probably infatuation, but whatever it was I'm over it and starting afresh. If you want to live the high life you'll need to get a job or whatever. Don't contact me again, and have a nice life with Eddie. Goodbye.'

Two little spots of red appeared on her cheeks and she hissed at him, 'I was a fool to marry you! My mother warned me that you weren't good enough and now you've broken my heart!'

Simon very much doubted that she actually had a heart to be broken, and despite being brought up properly he decided to end all the wheedling and untiring demands for more and more cash once and for all. He folded his arms and looked her straight in the eye, 'Well, we've both learnt from the experience then; and I'm sure your mother is as delighted as I am that we're divorcing.'

Jenn pursed her lips, turned on her heels and flounced back up the *chemin* as quickly as her towering heels would allow. About half-way up the slope she wobbled as she slipped on the loose calcaire. Not quite the cool and indignant exit she'd planned, Simon smiled. She tossed her blonde hair as she passed Émilie Fournier, who had stood watching the whole drama with some amusement, and disappeared from sight.

'That was *quite* a show!' Émilie called down to him. 'If there is to be another episode, please tell me and I will bring a chair and popcorn!' she snorted and disappeared back to the *boulangerie*. Obviously airing your dirty linen in public was not the done thing in France, he mused, but was secretly amused at her annoyed reaction.

***

Women! Simon reflected on them as he placed the fruit trees in the shade of the tool shed. They *had* to be a different species from men, he muttered to himself. They always had a way of reducing men to confused idiocy, and he'd never understand them. He was relieved that he and Jenn were finally divorcing after just a year of marriage. He couldn't believe that he'd fallen for the high maintenance, selfish airhead that she'd turned out to be. It had been a serious error of judgement on his part, but thankfully, there were no children involved. There'd been fault on both sides he acknowledged; him working too many hours and neglecting the marriage, but she had been the one that strayed, falling for the dubious charms and money of Simon's former glazing contractor.

It would have been funny if it hadn't meant an acrimonious split, with her engaging an infamous local divorce lawyer in order to *take him to the cleaners;* he recalled her saying when she'd returned to their flat to collect her belongings. As the pretty mask slipped from her face, he'd seen her true nature as she reduced their brief marriage into material things and scornful remarks. Funny how women started off looking adorable; even stunning, and then; after even a short time could be seen to change; the softness replaced with hard lines, the doe-like eyes turning glassy and empty; smiles becoming fixed and almost sneer-like.

And, not content with the generous settlement he'd agreed to in spite of his solicitor's warning; she'd come here, trying to milk more money from him. He shook his head, and sighed. It would be a *long* time before he entered into another relationship, no matter how enticing the inducement. He looked briefly at the spot where Émilie had just stood and then firmly turned back to the trees he'd bought. Work. Work was the answer. Work and more work was all he needed right now, and he'd start by planting the fruit trees.

***

The fan-trained pear was easy. He knew it would look fabulous on the south-facing wall of the mill, with the support and heat helping to nurture it, and in a year or so ripen the luscious fruits that would soon cover it. He dug a large hole, and gently planted the tree in place, firming it in with his boot. A trickle of water would be all that was needed today, after the flooding, but he'd keep an eye on watering during the fierce heat of the fast-approaching summer. Then he carried the spade and the two cherries to the spot where the *chemin* came down from the road and entered the future car parking area. The nurseryman had explained that they would grow quite large, so he planted each one on either side, about a metre from the edge of the chemin, staking them and ensuring the plastic deer protector was in place. The apples and the Mirabelle plum he intended for the far side of the leat, but he'd have to wait for the soil to drain for another day or two before he attempted to plant them, so he popped the spade back into the tool shed. He was finished for the day, but uneasy to leave the place.

The attempt to sabotage the project and destroy the work done on the cottage and mill had disturbed him greatly, and he was torn between staying in the cottage and returning to the scant comforts of Madame Cholet's bedroom of torture. He walked across the road to the bar and ordered a takeaway pizza and bottle of wine. Marie understood immediately, 'You will stay in the cottage tonight?' she asked as she boxed the pizza for him.

'I think I must or I will just worry,' he smiled, 'But I have the solar shower and some electricity, and…'

'And your own bed will be more comfortable than that of Madame Cholet?' Marie grinned, handing him the pizza box and bottle of red wine, '*Bon appétit*, and *bon soirée*, Simon. Try not to worry, life can only get better.'

Madame Cholet's bed must be infamous, he thought as he carried the meal back to the cottage. He sat outside and ate facing the millpond. After the attempted sabotage he tried to marshal the many thoughts competing for attention in his head. Had he *really* been mistaken that he could integrate into life in this village and become accepted or was he kidding himself? Would this be the final attempt to test his resolve or was it the start of a campaign to oust him? He sighed. Only time would tell, and he couldn't leave the project he had started at this crucial time. He'd invested too much money and much of himself in it to throw in the towel yet. He looked around at the amount of work he'd already done. The buildings *were* responding to the renovations. He recalled the conversation he'd had previously with Claude and Jojo; and agreed. And many of the villagers had come unbidden to his aid; many of whom he had previously not known. He smiled and relaxed, taking the final slice of pizza in his hand, and washing it down with another glass of excellent red wine. In the long grass on the opposite side of the mill pond some frogs were singing loudly. Well, perhaps not *singing*, but certainly communicating and loudly.

The geese were grazing quietly along the far bank of the leat and a couple of coots were herding their small chicks in and out of the irises and bulrushes at the far side of the pond. It certainly was an idyllic spot, he thought, enjoying the reflections of various shades of green on the pond surface. It was now the end of May, and he visualised the completed mill and cottage some time in the near future, alive with lights and smoke curling from the chimney. A romantic and picture-book scene that was some months, a lot of work and a fair amount of cash away, he told himself sternly and poured a final glass of wine.

In the cottage itself, apart from his bed and the small donated table under the window he had a couple of temporary sockets and a single light bulb hanging from the ceiling in what would eventually be the living room, but now sufficed to serve as his bedroom. At least the bed was long enough for his body and the mattress didn't bite into his back the way Madame Cholet's waffle-iron mattress had done. He smiled at the memory, pulled the duvet around his chin and fell fast asleep.

He woke with the bells of the church. He was pleased to note that they weren't as loud as they were in Madame Cholet's rental room; and he lay comfortable and warm listening to the gentle fall of water from the leat into the race, where sometime in the future a new wheel would be located. He could hear the geese honking gently on the far side of the meadow and the chirruping of frogs which seemed very loud and near. Slowly he got out of bed and dressed before throwing open the old front door. The sun was shining and it promised to be another hot day; the sky a liquid azure without a cloud, and he walked up the *chemin* and made his way to the *boulangerie*.

Swallows swooped and called to each other as he waited behind a very old lady who was buying baguettes. Émilie had her hair tied back, and was wearing a thin white cotton top and shorts. Her face was flushed as she carried a tray of croissants and *pains au chocolat* from the oven to load the baskets on the counter. Simon's mouth was watering and he was aware that the inducement wasn't just the sight of the pastries. He asked for two of each and two baguettes and popped them into his bag as he paid the baker. Eloise lay sprawled across the floor, beating her tangled tail as she recognised him.

'So, what are you doing today?' Émilie asked archly. 'Is your *wife* coming back to see you?'

'No, that's finished and I think she finally got the message yesterday,' he smiled. 'Today, I'm going to buy some curtains for the cottage, so I think it's a shopping trip to Périgueux to the large brico shop there.'

Her eyes lit up, and he smiled. Like every other woman he knew, shopping for home comforts was something they adored. 'I'm going about eleven, if you want to come,' he volunteered.

She looked downcast for a second, and then recovered, 'If you can wait till twelve, I can close then and come with you.'

'Well, alright. I'll go back home, do some measurements, make a list and we'll go at twelve.'

The *rendezvous* sorted, he returned to the cottage, made some coffee and ate the fresh, flaky pastries and waved to the workmen arriving. The radio was playing as the men began to lift in the flooring and insulation for the upper story of the mill and Simon left them to it, returning to measure the windows in the cottage for rails and curtains. He poured another coffee as he flicked through the catalogue of kitchen units and folded over the pages of the styles he liked. A catalogue photo was one thing, but he would see them in the flesh that afternoon, and Émilie would no doubt have an opinion on what would look best in the cottage. He was interrupted by a lorry arriving with the new oak staircase and spent the rest of the morning helping the workmen carry the structure into the shed, where it would have to lay until the carpenters had fully installed the upper floor of the mill. It rested on some wooden batons, just in case there was any residual dampness, and he just had time to change into his chinos and a clean shirt when Émilie arrived to smirks and murmurs from the men, who had now stopped for lunch. She laughed them off confidently, explaining that Simon needed an adequate translator and that she needed the opportunity to shop.

***

They left the men to their work, and drove up through Les Eyzies and on towards Périgueux and the many hardware suppliers and décor shops. Choosing the kitchen had been pretty straightforward, with Émilie pointing out that contemporary was easier to clean, more attractive to French gite guests, and would complement the traditional stone walls of the cottage. The units and integrated white goods were ordered, and they then visited the décor shop next door where curtain rails, roller blinds and curtains were also bought. He had baulked at Émilie's choice of lime green for the soft furnishings and insisted on sky blues and touches of yellow. She wrinkled her nose, 'So English!' she scoffed.

'Well, I *am* English, and anyway, it's *my* house. And those *lampshades*…absolutely useless!'

She laughed, 'but they are *chic*.'

'No chance. We'll try another shop,' he insisted and they spent another hour searching for suitable lighting. He eventually found something he liked in the very last shop which she kindly agreed were acceptable, and they returned to the village with a pickup stuffed with items, companionably tired and happy.

As they unloaded the car he thanked her, and ran a hand through his hair, 'Look, tonight I'm taking the Cholets out for dinner, to thank them for helping me; but if you are free tomorrow evening, we could try dinner at a nice little place in Urval, if you'd like.'

The invitation marked a change in their relationship; or would if she would agree. He caught himself holding his breath, waiting for her answer.

She smiled, 'The Veilleur? It's delightful; yes that would be very nice.' She lowered her eyes, the thick lashes grazing her dimpling cheeks and then walked back up the chemin and around the corner to the *boulangerie* with her own purchases, leaving him to stare just a fraction too long, before he shook himself and returned to the cottage to wash quickly and get ready to collect his friends for the meal out.

***

As he lay in his bed later that night he reflected on his good fortune. The building works were progressing, the weather had stayed dry, he seemed to be accepted by most of the villagers; and during his meal with the Cholet's he noted with pleasure that the pronoun *vous* had changed to the more informal *tu*, indicating a subtle but important change in their relationship, and Madame Cholet invited him to call her Josiane. It heralded the start of a friendship, and he'd have to learn to use the new pronoun *vu*. As he routinely spoke English with Émilie, his command of the French language had never come up as a problem, but he hoped *their* relationship was also progressing to a deeper friendship. He was looking forward to their dinner the following night, he realised with a grin. She was pretty, clever and amusing, and he wanted to find out more about her. So much for his avoiding complicated relationships, he thought as he got up to close the window against the frog chorus outside. He'd never known frogs to croak so loud! He'd mentioned them to Philippe at dinner and he'd smiled and would come in the morning to assess the problem, and propose a solution. If croaking frogs were the only problem he had to deal with at the moment he was quite happy, he thought and closed his eyes.

Chapter 6

They stood and listened together at the leat leaving the millpond. The croaking was incredibly loud, almost like a crowd of people talking loudly or low level machinery.

Philippe shrugged his shoulders, 'You live at a mill; there is water. Of *course* there are frogs.'

'But there must be hundreds of them!' Simon groaned, 'And they're so *loud*!'

Philippe searched for a moment in the grassy verge and caught one of the culprits.

'Common edible frogs.'

'Edible? Will the geese eat them?'

'No, geese are vegetarian, my friend. The egrets and herons will take a few but they are shy and you are making a lot of noise. I have an idea, but it will only reduce the population and not get rid of them completely.'

Simon nodded, 'Anything. The more we can get rid of the better I'll sleep!'

'I will put a notice in the *mairie*. *Cuisses de grenouille* is a French delicacy, and it is legal to collect as long as it is not commercial. If you are agreeable to people coming to collect them; perhaps early in the morning and at dusk?'

Simon shook his hand and Philippe left him, both men keen to begin their busy day.

By mid-afternoon word had obviously spread and a couple of older ladies appeared with a sack and began to search the banks of the leat both above and below the *étang*. They left about an hour later with a distinct bulge in the sack and lots of smiles and waves.

Simon shuddered. Whilst he was keen to embrace French life and cuisine, the idea of eating frogs' legs didn't appeal one bit. And what happened to the rest of the frog, he wondered uncomfortably.

***

At the end of the day he showered, and changed. Jojo had stayed behind with a bucket with a cloth draped over the top and was collecting a few of the green choir to take home for his mother; who apparently was mad for the tasty delicacy. He spent a few minutes explaining to Simon the best way to kill and skin the frogs and remove their little legs whilst Simon forced a smile on his face and waved him off. He'd been repulsed at the process and was reminding himself of the main event of the evening - dinner with the delectable Émilie.

She appeared at half past six in a simple floral dress and her hair tied back with a pink ribbon. Simon took a moment to appreciate the pretty woman, and opened the pickup door for her.

'I hope this is going to be nice', he said, trying to cover his excitement with small-talk. 'All I've heard all day is how frogs' legs are a delicacy, and I have mixed feelings about dinner.'

She laughed, 'The Veilleur is a real treat. It's been a few years since I ate there, but has a good reputation, and I've never known frogs' legs to be on the menu.'

They drove down through the countryside skirting the Dordogne River, and soon arrived in Urval, and parked opposite the small restaurant. They chose to eat outside to enjoy the weather and the warmth and were soon discussing the menu excitedly. They both ordered the same, salmon gravalax with local cider and a glass each of a crisp white Chardonnay, and then a lamb tajine with local plums. The waiter suggested a glass of the local red Bergerac wine to accompany the main course, and when Simon hesitated; he disappeared inside and

60

reappeared with the bottle.

'Try it' he suggested and poured a small amount.

Simon raised the glass and sniffed. Bergerac red had a reputation for being the poor relation to the more prestigious wines from Bordeaux, but this little wine he tasted was no also-ran. It had a beautiful flavour and smoothness with a hint of blackberries and vanilla in the finish. He smiled at the waiter and asked for a bottle, 'If we don't finish it here, we can take it home,' he smiled to Émilie.

They laughed and chatted, and flirted a little too as they ate and learned a little more about each other. The sun dipped and Émilie pulled on her lambs' wool cardigan and they waited for the restaurant speciality – the fondant chocolate dessert.

Simon couldn't remember the last time he'd had such a good meal and with such pleasant company. After coffee and promising to return very soon, they drove back to St Honoré as the sky began to fill with stars. Reluctantly he walked her back home, wishing he didn't have to say goodnight; not just yet.

'That was a wonderful evening, thank you,' Émilie said and kissed his cheek. Simon waited till she closed the door of the *boulangerie* before returning to the cottage. He realised he was in danger of falling head over heels with Madame Fournier, and made himself a strong coffee. Not very bright to embark on a romance when both parties were still actually married, he told himself severely. He stood outside and looked up at the stars. With a pretty girl, a wonderful meal in a beautiful country and a whole galaxy of stars above him it would be very hard *not* to fall in love, he smiled.

The frogs sang their own serenade loudly as he went back inside and closed the door. Philippe had said the mating season could last until mid-June, so he would need to be patient and hope that the villagers kept returning to harvest his noisy residents. As the summer became hotter, he'd need to start sleeping with the window open and the repetitive croaking would prevent him from dreaming of the delectable Émilie.

***

Not all the village slept however. Jacques was armed with a torch and a bucket and searching the banks of the stream for frogs. That was his *legitimate* excuse if anyone saw him, but he had a much more sinister reason for creeping towards the mill. Inside his pocket he had secreted a sharp needle. He'd seen the Englishman arrive home and waited a good hour after the lights went off in the cottage before creeping towards the parked pickup.

Inside him a battle was underway. Whilst he was desperate to fix the Englishman at any cost to force him to leave the mill, the weight of the guilt and possibility of discovery was making him ill. The villagers knew that he was responsible for the flooding incident and he'd had to face many looks of disgust from people he'd known since he was a boy. At the *Salamandre*, Henri and Marie had made it clear that whilst they were not banning him, they were no longer happy with his custom, and he was now forced to drive to St Cyprien to drink at the bar on the main road, which increased the risk of being stopped by the *gendarmes*.

***

Now that the mill was being renovated he could no longer take advantage of the chance to search it at his leisure. He was convinced that old Renauld, who had lived at the mill until his sudden death ten years ago, had been telling him the truth about his secret stash of money, hidden somewhere in the mill. Many old people didn't trust banks and still kept metal boxes with money and valuables hidden in the house. Before his death, Renauld had shared a bottle of *pastis* with the artist and his loose tongue had divulged that he himself had the *perfect* hiding place for his valuables in the mill. Jacques had been instantly alert, but the old man, realising he'd said too much, clammed up immediately and staggered home. A few weeks later a sudden massive heart attack had seen him off, and Jacques watched as the inevitable visits by family emptied the house of the meagre furnishings and possessions and the mill was left empty and eventually put up for sale. He'd spent many a night with his flashlight unsuccessfully searching the rooms and the attic of the mill house, cottage and sheds. Then catastrophe! The mill was sold and before the new owner appeared, Jacques searching became more intense, but still fruitless.

His bitterness increased and his hatred grew for the unsuspecting foreigner trying to carve out a new life for himself. He'd seen the workers replacing the joists and roof of the buildings and nothing had been found. The old staircase had now been replaced and they were about to start work on the stone floor and Jacques was almost beside himself. If they hadn't discovered the hiding place by now, it *must* be discovered soon. He was running out of time and had to stop the Englishman. Flooding hadn't put him off and now Jacques had been forced to employ a more permanent solution.

***

With a black balaclava hiding his face he slowly and quietly wriggled under the car and carefully located the brake pipes. He took the needle and pushed it slowly in, creating one tiny hole, then a second nearby. With his heart hammering and his hands shaking, he replaced the needle into his pocket and wriggled back out, before gleefully retracing his steps back towards his own cottage with the empty bucket. He was gasping for a cigarette and lit one whilst pouring a tumbler of *eau de vie* with his trembling hands. He was delighted with himself, dancing manically in circles round his studio, sending the feral cat into a frenzy trying to escape away from the madman. It was a few hours before he managed to drink himself to sleep, dreaming of sinister shadows and faces long dead.

Simon tossed and turned in his own bed, his own dreams ranging from macabre legless frogs pulling themselves along the verge by the stream, to tantalising and fleeting glimpses of Émilie Fournier's legs accompanied by laughter which weirdly turned into croaking. Then the legless frogs were suddenly in wheelchairs, wheeling themselves up and down the slope of the *chemin* singing into microphones like some ludicrous choir. At seven he awoke in a sweat, untangled himself from the duvet and got up, throwing the windows open to chase the dreams away.

He was pleased to see some more villagers with sacks or buckets, all poking around the meadow and banks of the stream, and walked around to the *boulangerie* to get his morning pastries.

There were knowing smiles and nudges from a couple of the older ladies in the queue, and he was aware of Émilie's blushes, but he just smiled and brazened it out. Honestly – it was just a meal with a friend! Loaded up with *pains au chocolat* and baguettes he returned home and met with the workmen. Today the woodburner was being installed in the cottage, so he needed to move the bed to its final location in the upstairs bedroom. This meant dismantling it, and he and Claude spent an hour doing this and re-assembling it in the brand new bedroom, whilst Mr Durand made a great fuss of unloading and preparing the woodburner itself. Simon decided to leave him to it, telling Claude to keep an eye on him and hitched up the trailer to the pick-up and drove to Sarlat to collect some more furniture from the storage unit. It was already warm as he drove towards the town. There was a stop-start line of traffic heading into the old medieval centre and he skirted around the periphery of the town to the unit.

On his way back, his dashboard almost immediately lit up with an orange warning light and simultaneously the pick-up went into limp mode. He was only ten minutes from St Honoré and decided to drive very slowly back to the garage at St Cyprien. So, with hazard lights on and impatient drivers honking their horns at him, he eventually arrived at the garage just before twelve. He explained as best he could about the warning light and was told to leave the vehicle, they'd put it on the diagnostic machine after lunch. Simon groaned. His trailer was full of furniture which he didn't want to leave unattended whilst the garage staff had their two-hour lunch break, so he got his mobile phone out, found the number for the *Salamandre* and explained his dilemma to Henri, who agreed to come out and rescue him.

Back home he unhitched the trailer, thanked Henri profusely and on the spur of the moment joined the other workers at the terrace table for lunch. He was unsettled and annoyed at the sudden problem with the pick-up. He'd had an MOT and a full service done before leaving the UK and was mystified at the breakdown. Hopefully, in the afternoon the garage would have some answers for him, and a not too expensive remedy. He ate slowly, enjoying the company of the men who were beginning to become his friends, and his anxiety had all but disappeared when his *tarte tatin* appeared. Jojo offered to take him back to the garage later in the afternoon, and they made their way back to the mill after a leisurely lunch.

He admired the new woodburner, now all connected to the flue liner, and the instructions left by Mr Durand. As the woodburner was new, he must light it and let it burn *all night* to burn off the chemicals and ensure the chimney and flue were all working perfectly. He would return in the morning to sign it off. Simon groaned; it was already 27 degrees and sleeping in a cottage with a lit woodburner was not a night he was looking forward to. He moved the furniture in and put up the curtain poles and curtains he'd bought on his shopping trip with Émilie. By the end of the afternoon, it was beginning to look homely, and with this cheery thought, he summoned Jojo to visit the garage.

The technician was serious and spoke in rapid French which Jojo translated. The machine had indeed found the fault; leaking brake pipes, and new ones were on order. Normally they would arrive the next day or the day after, he indicated with a Gallic wiggle of his hand. Simon groaned inwardly; he'd have to leave the car there. But the technician wasn't finished. The damage was very odd. He'd noticed the oily brake fluid on the underside and when the pipes had been removed he'd been curious as they appeared to be in good condition. Simon was listening intently. Warming to his theme and with a rapt audience the technician announced he had detected one tiny hole, then another, which amazed him as the pipe showed no other sign of wear and tear.

'Are you saying the holes were made *deliberately*?' Simon demanded.

This was rather too direct for the technician who became a little flustered.

Jojo turned to Simon, 'He doesn't want to say this. If it was an old car you would quickly have no brakes working, which could be fatal. Because your car is modern, you had the safety feature of the limp mode.'

As Simon's face registered his horror the technician nodded, and indicated he would call Simon's mobile when the car was fixed.

Jojo pulled Simon back to his own car, and they drove in silence back to the mill.

Jojo parked up and immediately rounded the others up. A short, but animated discussion drew Simon's attention, but when he approached the others they went quiet and returned to their work. They worked till six and stopped to tidy the tools away, before waving goodbye. It appeared that no-one was going to the *Salamandre* this evening, so Simon; at a loss for something to do, made-up and lit the woodburner and once it was burning well, carried a plastic chair out of the shed and sat outside his cottage, going through the emails on his laptop.

The crunch of footsteps on the calcaire *chemin* interrupted his concentration and he looked up to see Émilie striding crossly towards him.

'Claude says you have no car, that it is in the garage and you are fortunate to be alive.' She stood in front of him, arms crossed and formidable.

He closed the laptop and tried to calm her down, 'Now Émilie, the car is getting fixed…'

'Claude says the technician says maybe someone has done something to the brakes?'

'Well, he thinks he might have found a hole, but really…'

She looked around crossly for another chair, and he leaped to his feet, offering his chair as he pulled another from the shed. She flounced before sitting.

'Why are you not angry? Claude says all the men say it must be Jacques again! You must tell the *gendarmes*!'

Simon took her hands and tried to soothe her, 'Look, I'm the outsider here. Yes, *maybe* someone tampered with the car; maybe it was Jacques, although I doubt he has the knowledge, and perhaps it was just natural. The car will be fine, *I'm* fine, and there is no proof anyone did anything. I just need to keep my eyes open from now on.'

She pulled her hands free from his and blushed. 'Maybe you need to get a dog. A *big* dog.'

He laughed and ran his hand through his hair, 'No dogs! But I *will* be careful. When I get the car back, I'll park it right outside the cottage. And I'll get some security lights too.'

She smiled and turned to walk back up the chemin, 'Okay, no dog, but maybe you need to get a gun in case that …that *sous-merde* tries anything else!'

He watched her stomp off and smiled. He didn't have a clue what a *sous-merde* was, Jojo would no doubt enlighten him, but that little exchange showed that perhaps Émilie liked him more than he'd previously thought, and he was quite happy with that. He opened the shed door, pulled out a little garden table and then after a few minutes in the roasting cottage returned with a dish of olives, some bread and a bottle of *Pecharmant* wine. It was time for a glass of wine and to reflect on the day, and he sat in the sun, watching a pair of hoopoe's explore the grass under the new apple trees and relaxed. There was no point in going into the sweltering house; even with the windows flung open the heat from the woodburner was incredible and he resolved to sleep in the tool shed in his old sleeping bag, but for now he was content to sit outside with a glass of good wine and a few olives, and listen (as if he had any choice) to the frogs.

Chapter 7

The architect paid a brief visit and declared he was pleased at the progress. The cottage was coming along nicely and they could focus on some of the major works to be undertaken. Although they couldn't install solar panels on the roof because of the building's proximity to the church, there *were* ways of getting round the problem he indicated tapping the side of his nose. Siting the panels on the ground in a discreet area of the meadow would not detract from the historic importance of the mill and no-one would be able to see them from the village or road. He would personally complete the necessary paperwork, he assured Simon. It was perhaps time to take some photographs of the works completed and to get a little publicity to bring the locals and the departmental authorities on board, and he would write something for the local radio and the newspaper. This might encourage the local planners to see the merit in the works and to allow room for manoeuvre.

Meanwhile the kitchen units for the cottage arrived and Simon spent the next week installing the kitchen himself, with the help of the electricians and plumber.

Sudden summer storms in the late afternoon failed to cause any issues and by the next day the ground was dry and the *étang* and the leats were behaving. Jacques was largely absent from the village as he was reportedly attending the markets and brocantes attempting to sell his paintings, and Simon began to wonder if he was just the village scapegoat, who was in all probability totally innocent of any malice towards him. Village life revolved round ensuring the fields of sunflowers and wheat were watered and the hay crop to be brought in safely. The air hummed with the smell of sun ripened hay and the drone of tractors and farm machinery was a pleasant background noise.

Tourists began to arrive in ever growing numbers and the *Salamandre* was doing a roaring trade, resulting in difficulty getting a table for food in the evening, and Simon spent more time at the cottage itself. His fruit trees were looking a little dry and he ensured he watered them nightly. The tomatoes at the *boulangerie* garden were growing ever bigger and he and Émilie were both too busy to arrange another meal out.

The frog problem also seemed to have resolved itself; either the villagers had plundered enough to reduce the population considerably or the frogs were finished mating, but evenings started to become noticeably quieter. He'd fitted mosquito blinds to the cottage windows and was now sleeping every night with the windows open, and finally he stopped having dreams about disabled frogs in wheelchairs.

***

His father had called one evening, berating busy-body neighbours, and Simon decided perhaps it was time he returned to Bristol for a few days to see for himself what was going on. He arranged a schedule of work with the workmen for a few days and asked the Cholets to keep an eye on his place for him. Philippe drove him to the airport and the conversation revolved around the care of his father.

'Why not bring him back here for a week?'

'The cottage isn't ready yet, and we'd have to share a room right now,' Simon answered, 'I'll assess him when I'm there and see what the problem is with the neighbours; he's never fallen out with them before. Sadly, parents' age and I'll need to prepare for the inevitable.'

'I will keep an eye on the workers, but I'm sure everything will be okay for a few days. Call me and I'll come and collect you,' Philippe said at the airport, shaking his hand warmly,

'*Bon voyage, mon ami.*'

Simon dozed in the plane until the final approach to Bristol, and the descent through thick grey clouds. Nothing much had changed then, he noted, and slipped his jacket on as he walked to the car rental. It was strange to be driving on what he now considered the 'wrong' side of the road; and the volume of traffic and trucks reminded him of one of the reasons he had left the city. As he drew up to his father's house, he was dismayed by the sight of the garden which was overgrown and uncared for. With a sigh he pulled his bag from the car and walked to the door.

His father was of course delighted to see him, and Simon was relieved to see that the house was reasonably warm, but a bit untidy. He agreed to a cup of tea and busied himself in the small kitchen, noting that the fridge could have been fuller and that there seemed to be too few dirty dishes in the sink. On an impulse he took them out for lunch, and enjoyed watching his father demolish a roast chicken dinner as he told him about France and the mill.

It was only on their return to the house that Simon saw the neighbour's curtains open and Sally; his dad's long-term neighbour signal furiously that she'd like to talk to him. Settling his dad in a chair he nipped next door.

'I'm so glad to see you', she said, hugging him.

He threw himself into an armchair as she began to tell him her worries.

'We don't think he's eating much as he goes out so seldom, and he's becoming a bit of a recluse. He used to let me in to help him do the hovering or hang out heavy washing, but that's almost stopped and he's not visiting his friends at the library or the bowling club any more. I don't know if he's ill or just lonely, but he's *changed* since you left.'

Simon sighed. His sixth sense had been right and something was amiss then. Now it seemed the relationship between parent and child was reversing and it was his turn to try and look after his fiercely independent father. That wouldn't be easy, he realised, or quick.

'I'll be here a few days then I have to get back, but I'll take him shopping this evening and tomorrow I'll cut the grass and tidy the garden. If I spend a bit more time with him, I'll maybe get to the bottom of it, Sally.'

She stared at him sadly, aware of just how hard this was going to be, and acknowledging the fact that Simon had his own life away from his father. She didn't envy him dealing with the increasingly difficult situation.

Back in the house he went through the cupboards and fridge, making a shopping list, and noticing the vast store of medicine in one of the cupboards. It was time for a serious chat, he realised as he saw that the dates on the medicine were months old.

Andrew Parker was a quiet man, independent since his wife had died many years before and didn't relish his son taking him to task about how he was living. He grudgingly accepted he'd let the garden slide a little and even agreed to Simon organising and paying to have the grass cut weekly, but the real resistance came when Simon mentioned going together to visit his doctor.

'Look dad, I'm not going to be living here and I'd just like to look after you, and know you're okay. You've not been eating and *definitely* not taking your medicine regularly. I can see that by what's in the cupboards! I'm not asking you to change your life, but I need to know *why* there's been this sudden change. Sally's really worried about you and I am too.'

'You're not going to make me go into a home or somewhere, I'm *not* doolally, you know!' his father flared.

'No one said you were, but this medication has been lying a while, so let's just get a check-up, eh?'

The argument went on for about an hour before Andrew finally capitulated and allowed Simon to make the appointment.

Whilst on the phone to the doctor's receptionist, Simon explained that he was only in the UK for a few days and that he was very concerned, and asked for emergency appointment the next day; whilst his father listened and rolled his eyes angrily and blustered a little. After this they went shopping, with Simon noting his father's hesitance at the supermarket, and confusion over some of the things in the trolley. The short shopping trip turned into an ordeal, and it was almost dinner time when they returned. As Simon unloaded and filled the fridge and cupboards, Andrew napped in the chair. Feeling a little guilty, Simon took advantage of his father sleeping and began to rummage quietly in the drawers of the sideboard. Unopened letters and bills had been shoved in and the drawers were almost overflowing. He took a handful into the kitchen and began to open them. Final demands for the electricity and phone bill and a letter from the insurance company confirming the cancellation of the house insurance alarmed him. He called them all on his mobile and once he'd negotiated the usual automated service paid the unpaid bills and reinstated the house insurance, setting up direct debits for the future. Then he began to peel some potatoes and made some cottage pie for them both. His father woke at seven, disorientated and surprised to see Simon,

'Did you come straight from work?' he asked.

'No dad, I've been here since lunchtime.'

'Oh yes, I remember now.'

'I've paid the bills now and sorted a direct debit for them; it'll be easier for me to manage them.'

His father didn't question this, and instead of explaining he'd found and paid the bills he breezily added that it was cottage pie for dinner. There was no point in telling the poor man off for something that he wasn't able to process, and he was trying to maintain a positive atmosphere rather than have his father totally set against accepting that he needed help.

That night Simon lay in his childhood bed. The room smelt stale and damp and he was uneasy and overtired. Maybe he'd been expecting too much from the visit. After all, during his brief marriage to Jenn, they had only visited on Sundays and birthdays and he hadn't noticed his father ageing. Then after the break-up he'd visited less frequently, overwhelmed with selling the apartment and his business and the divorce. It was life; getting in the way and pushing out the failing relationship with his father and he felt guilty and depressed. Had he just run away to France to escape his failed marriage and his unravelling life in England? The answer was of course yes, he acknowledged that, but he also realised that in the past months in France he was happier; he'd appeared to find contentment and happiness working on the old mill and living a quieter and more meaningful life. For the first time since leaving France, he realised he was missing the place; badly. Images of the mill, the bar, the beautiful landscape and the beautiful Ms Fournier darted through his mind, and he longed to be back. But first, he had to deal with the issues surrounding his father. He rolled over and pulled the duvet around him and sleep eventually gave his troubled mind some respite.

The next morning after a fractious breakfast and excuses not to go from his father, they arrived at the doctor's surgery. The middle-aged GP welcomed them both in and after a brief explanation from Simon, immediately began to review his notes on Andrew Parker. He posed a few random questions to Andrew and then suggested a visit to a geriatric consultant, which had Andrew bristling and cross.

'It's just a check-up,' he smiled. 'Anyone over the age of seventy is considered a geriatric now, it's nothing personal. I'm almost one myself', he smiled, trying to placate the old man.

He passed the card to Simon with an appointment just two weeks away. 'I'd like to screen any obvious infections with a urine sample' he said, handing a small vial to Andrew, 'there's a toilet just outside.'

As Andrew momentarily left the room, the doctor took the opportunity to have a brief, confidential chat with Simon.

'You think he has dementia, I assume?' The doctor was

blunt, but hitting the nail on the head, Simon thought as he nodded.

'Well, he's the right age, and lonely; and from what you've told me, it could well be, but let's take it a step at a time. There's medication which can help, but the consultant will do some cognitive tests and we'll have a proper diagnosis. Sadly, it's more common as the population live longer, and he and you will have to make some lifestyle changes. You're just at the start of an unpleasant journey, I'm afraid.' He broke off as Andrew returned with the little vial discreetly wrapped in toilet paper.

'I'll send this off today, and see you after your appointment with the consultant, Mr Parker. Meantime, enjoy your time with your son, and let him spoil you a little.'

***

Back at the house, Simon got the lawnmower out and began to mow the lawn. His father was making them both lunch and Simon left him to it, only returning to the kitchen to wash his hands. Tea was waiting and Simon raised the cup to his lips, only to find that the water was stone cold. He threw the 'tea' down the sink, filled and this time ensured the kettle was boiling before making them both fresh cups. Ham sandwiches were devoured and Simon sat down to broach the future with his father.

'I'll come back the night before the appointment with the consultant, and we can see what he says, dad,' he began.

'Well, I feel fine, and I can go on my own. It's only in the city centre.'

'No, I'll go with you, just so we both understand what's going on.'

His father frowned, 'But you're busy, and anyway, Jenn can take me.'

'*Jenn* can take you?' Simon exclaimed with a sinking heart. What on earth was he thinking?

75

'Yes, she comes to see me sometimes and brings me some chocolates.'

Simon was concerned at this. Jenn had never been keen on going to visit Andrew when they'd been married, but visiting him now seemed outlandish.

'Dad, you *do* remember that Jenn and I are getting a divorce? When was the last time she came here?'

'She was here about a week ago. Silly girl was in a state about an unpaid bill, so she took me to the cash point in the High Street and I gave her money to pay it.'

'Dad, Jenn is getting half of the house I sold here, and shouldn't be asking *you* for money!' Simon exclaimed, furious that his father had been used in such a cavalier way.

Andrew stared at his son, uncomprehending, 'But she said it was all just a misunderstanding and that she still loved you…'

'*No*, Dad. Jenn was having an *affair*. *She* left me; there was no 'misunderstanding'.'

He was angry, but his dad just looked confused, and suddenly oh so old. His heart was suddenly too full and he got up out of his chair and squeezed his dad's shoulder, 'It's fine. But she's *not* to come back here, and you've not to give her any money.'

His father crumpled in the chair, lost in a world Simon felt he couldn't penetrate. He made them some fresh tea and told his father he was popping next door to see Sally.

After explaining about the visit to the doctor and the appointment with the consultant he tried to get some more information from Sally.

'Dad mentioned Jenn has been to see him. Do you know anything about that or is he imagining it?'

'Oh yes, *she* was here,' Sally frowned, 'but didn't stay long. I think she took him out in the car, but was back shortly afterwards. I gave her a piece of my mind as she was leaving, but I have no idea what it was about.'

'She took him to get money from the cash point; some story about being unable to pay a bill. I'll get my solicitor onto it and get an injunction against her if possible, but keep your eyes open Sally. Look; I have to go back in a day or so, but obviously we have a situation here. If dad has dementia then I'll need to think of a permanent solution. I think we need to wait and see what the consultant says, and I know it's a big ask – but could you keep a close eye on him until I come back?'

Sally threw her arms round him, 'Of course love! I'll even look at what there is locally in the way of sheltered housing and let you know, although, between you and me, I think he's gone beyond that and it's a care home he needs now.'

The same thoughts had been occurring to Simon, and he left Sally's, pausing outside his dad's house to have a private phone call with his solicitor, who was shocked and agreed to immediately write to the almost divorced Mrs Parker, and to apply to the courts for an injunction.

Simon pushed the door open to the house and tried to be objective. He only had two more days before he had to return to France and he needed to make the most of them, trying to sort his dad's unravelling life. The next day would have to be spent doing a huge pile of laundry, and attending to small jobs round the house. He'd also contact the friends who Andrew refused to see, and invite them over to try and rekindle some sort of social life for the confused man, who was sitting watching TV.

This once strong man, capable and clever, funny and supportive was disintegrating in front of him. The roles were reversing and he knew it was his time to pick up the role of carer and to try and provide for the health and well-being of his remaining parent. He opened his laptop and began to research dementia. It made for grim reading, and he realised that the doctor had been correct – he really was in for an unpleasant journey and he was only just starting out along the road. Not for the first time, he wished he was back in France in the sun, listening to the gurgling water and even the damn frogs. He wondered sadly if Émilie was missing him at all.

Chapter 8

The next morning arrived with hazy sunshine as Simon filled the washing machine with the first of three loads of his father's clothes; and as doing the laundry would take up the whole morning, he began to telephone Andrew's friends. It became clear from the conversations that there had been some misunderstandings, and Simon arranged for his closest friends, Ted and Elliot to meet them both at his dad's old bowling club that lunchtime. He remembered that both his parents had been members and that his father had been a good bowler just a few years back.

So, with the final load in the machine and his dad actually looking forward to the lunch, they headed off in the hire car.

It cheered Simon up considerably as he sat listening to his dad and his friends chatting and laughing together over a light lunch. The recent misunderstandings all being forgotten now, they got on like a house on fire and offered to collect Andrew the following Tuesday for a game at the club. Whilst thanking them, Simon mentioned that Andrew had been unwell, and the renewed friendship was very welcome. He also gave both men his card with his mobile number and email address on it, asking them to keep an eye on his dad whilst he was away. Ted took him aside at the bar whilst Simon paid the lunch bill.

'It's dementia isn't it?' he asked bluntly, and without waiting for Simon to reply continued, 'He's been a bit off for the last couple of months, claiming the neighbour was stealing money and people were spying on him. My Betty had it. At the start of it she was just like he is now. It was horrible at the end; she didn't even know who I was.'

He saw the troubled look on Simon's face and grasped his forearm, 'I'll keep tabs on him for you, lad. Luckily I still seem to have all my marbles; at least for the moment.'

***

In the afternoon whilst Andrew napped, Simon hung out the last load of laundry. Sally looked over the fence and he confided that Ted was going to call on Tuesday to take Andrew to the Bowling Club.

'I'm going back tomorrow morning. It can't be helped, I need to get back,' he said. 'I'll come back the day before his appointment and try and stay as long as I can, but we'll need to think about future care. I think sheltered housing would have been ideal maybe a year ago, but not now. I'll see what I can organise at home; maybe he'd enjoy a long-term holiday in the sun, who knows.'

'I'll go in and see him every day, but you'll need to *tell* him that you said so. Having an argument with him is like going three rounds with a boxer – he don't pull no punches! Maybe I should slip him some happy pills, because he can be quite nasty when he wants, you know,' Sally answered folding her arms and looking as if she could easily best him in the ring.

'You've got my number, just call and I'll phone you back. And Sally – you're a star. Thank you,' he hugged her affectionately. 'And *no* happy pills; not yet.'

They sat that night with a can of beer each, watching the snooker on TV. Just like the old days, Andrew had said. Simon looked covertly at him. It was nothing like the old days, he thought. His dad was a shadow of the man he used to be, and Simon would have to try and make the rest of his life easier for him. As a result, he foresaw his own life in France suddenly changing. Instead of a new shiny adventure in the sun, there were now clouds on the horizon. It was up to him now to see how he could chase those clouds away. Work on the mill was progressing; and the cottage would be a proper habitable home in less than a month. With two bedrooms he could easily have his dad stay for some time. An extended holiday he'd said out loud to Sally. Why not? He'd make some enquiries with the pension people and see if his healthcare would be covered if he came to France. He popped into the kitchen and made them both toasted cheese. It had been a ritual when he was living at home; a little supper snack at the end of the evening. He passed the plate to him and was pleased to see his father grin back.

'What sort of cheese do they have where you are?' his father asked suddenly. It was the first time he'd asked anything about France and Simon described the local cheese,

'Well I tend to buy Cantal, which is the closest thing to cheddar, but there are loads of goats' cheeses locally. In fact, someone in my village makes goats' cheese and it's very nice. You should come over and try it and get a bit of sunshine.'

There. He'd suggested it. A visit to his new home. His father munched quietly and ignored the invitation, so Simon tried again.

'You know, I really could do with some advice regarding the main building. You were a builder before I was, so maybe you could help me decide how to do the renovation work. If you came out for a few days.'

He was really dangling the bait now, whilst trying not to make it too obvious, 'It's only an hour long flight, and we could fly out together next time I'm here.'

Andrew stopped chewing and appeared to be considering.

'Oh, I don't know son. I don't like to leave the house empty...'

'Sally'll keep an eye on the place, and it would just be for a few days. You and mum used to *love* to travel. I'm sure you've told me you'd visited Paris before. And I *really* could do with some pointers, you know...'

'Well, maybe. I'm not as young as I was, you know, and I'd be in the way...'

'Dad, if I didn't want you there, I wouldn't ask. Let's think more about it next time I'm here. Have you got a passport?'

'In the dresser drawer,' Andrew muttered waving a hand vaguely towards the oak dresser. Simon got up and began to rummage. Thankfully there were no more bills lying around, but he found an envelope stuffed with money, which a quick count amounted to £300. Eventually he found the passport, which thankfully had two years to run. He handed the envelope full of money to Andrew, 'This was in the drawer Dad. You said you'd had money stolen, didn't you?'

His father took the envelope and stared at his son, 'I must have put it in the drawer and forgotten. I thought Sally'd taken it. I'll need to apologise; God knows what she must think.' He ran a tired hand over his eyes.

'I'll explain to Sally before I go, but all the bills will be paid by direct debit now, so you don't need to have that kind of money in the house.'

The snooker having finished, Simon turned the TV off and took the plates to the kitchen, before following his dad upstairs.

The short visit had let him assess and sort some things out for his father, and right now he could do no more. But in this short visit fences had been mended, friendships rekindled and strengthened and his father was looking brighter than he had on Simon's arrival. He packed his small bag and when he got into his bed, fell asleep instantly.

***

Sally answered her door at 7am, looking like she'd been dragged through a hedge backwards. When she recognised him, she slammed the door to leave him standing outside in the drizzle whilst he listening to her pounding up the stairs yelling, 'Wait there till I put my teeth in!'

A few minutes later, she reappeared; hair brushed almost into place; and by the huge smile she bestowed on Simon, he saw that she had indeed found her dentures. He explained that he'd found the missing cash and apologised for his father's accusation.

'If you can just pop in maybe twice a day and check on him, I'll be back in a couple of weeks to take him to see the consultant. I have to get back to check on the contractors.'

'Send me a postcard,' she grinned, and planted a large wet kiss on his cheek, 'Now get off, and I'll make him a cuppa afterwards.'

He grabbed his bag and coat and threw them into the hire car whilst his dad looked on sadly. Sally had come out too and was holding her umbrella over them both. He turned to his dad and gave him a huge hug.

'I won't be too long, just over a week. I'll send you both a postcard to show you the area. Now Dad; behave for Sally, and I'll see you soon.' He forced himself to get in the car, anxious about leaving, but knowing he had to go. By the time he arrived at the airport and had returned the car, he felt a little better; and in the departure lounge amongst the tourists waiting to fly to Bergerac, the excitement was infectious and he was longing to get back to his little piece of paradise.

***

Bergerac Airport was bathed in sunshine. As they disembarked onto the tarmac, the air shimmered and he breathed deeply. He quickly made his way outside and saw Philippe, who hugged him and bestowed the Gallic *bisous* on both cheeks.

'It is good to see you! Everything is well?'

Simon nodded and climbed into the small Renault, and they began the hour long drive home. Home. He was delighted to be going home, and as they drove alongside the Dordogne River, Simon knew he had made the right decision moving to France.

They arrived late-afternoon and Philippe left him to catch up with the contractors. Marie shouted 'Cou-Cou' from the restaurant terrace of *La Salamandre,* and he shouted back to beg a table for that evening.

The men were slapping his back and welcoming him and all trying to show him what they had completed in his absence. He put them off till the next morning, but was touched by their welcome; and after an early supper and many questions at the bar, went straight to bed.

***

At the *boulangerie* the next morning all hell was breaking loose. He'd walked round to collect his usual order of bread and *pain au chocolat* and to see Émilie, but was dumbfounded to see the door closed and a few villagers milling around. The *maire's* little white van was parked outside together with an expensive looking black sports car, and the usually tranquil village square was resonating with shouting from within. Simon approached one elderly woman to find out what was going on, but she shook her head sadly and threw her hands in the air, murmuring something incomprehensible. Madame Cholet burst forth from the *boulangerie* door and with a look of embarrassment and despair, pushed past Simon,

'The husband has returned and is demanding to sell the place!' she finally said before returning to her own home.

Then the *maire* appeared, mopping his head and looking distraught, 'We may be losing our *boulangerie*', he told the crowd sadly as he got into his van, 'And I need to call a meeting of the committee.'

Nothing ever happens in the country, Simon said to himself. That was the usual saying, but whatever was going on in St. Honoré this morning, the village would be talking about it for days. Simon stood outside the church door, in the shade, watching to see what else was going to happen, worrying if Émilie was alright, and feeling generally confused and useless. The villagers began to walk away, gossiping and shaking their heads, leaving him the only obvious onlooker.

A tall thin man in a black shirt and trousers appeared suddenly, throwing the *boulangerie* door shut behind him in a fit of temper. He stared at Simon for a moment before getting into his car and screeching off out of the village. This kind of drama was better than anything on French TV, Simon thought.

Waiting for a few moments, Simon tentatively approached the door, which was unlocked. He called her name but receiving no reply he began to mount the old wooden stairs, calling her name again quietly.

He found her sitting on her bed. Her pretty face was red with crying and her hair loose and untidy. She raised her face to him and he saw that the man had slapped her. Fury filled him as he found the small bathroom, wet a flannel and returned to sit with her, wiping her tears away. He took her in his arms and held her till the sobbing ended, and then tactfully withdrew to give her a few minutes privacy. He walked downstairs to the back kitchen and tried to find a kettle. Eventually he found a *cafetiére* and some coffee and started to make some strong coffee.

She appeared eventually and sat in a chair, 'Thank you', she whispered, taking a long sip from the proffered mug.

'I'm assuming *that* was your husband?' Simon asked, 'and that he wants to sell the bakery?'

She nodded, 'He has found another woman, and wants the money from the *boulangerie* and a divorce, so I have no option but to agree to sell.'

'I'm so sorry,' he murmured. Inside he was furious. What could he say to this poor girl who was about to lose her home *and* livelihood, married to a violent bully? He tried to find the words, but they turned to ash in his mouth. Instead, he had to try and be a practical help to her.

'Do you have a lawyer?'

'I will call him shortly. I need to …compose myself.' she finished.

'I'll take you if you wish, just come and tell me what you want.'

She put the empty cup on the table and looked at him, 'I will have to sell, but the money I receive will perhaps pay for a small house, but I cannot have a house *and* a bakery. I'm finished. I will have to go and work for someone else.'

She was heartbroken and he felt useless.

A villager began tapping on the door, oblivious to the drama that had unfolded and the situation within. Émilie sighed, got up and went to the door; calling for the customer to wait a moment. She reappeared and pulled a hairbrush from her handbag, trying to coax her curling hair into submission and snapping a hair band to hold it in place. Simon felt it was time to go, and took her hand, 'I'll come back after lunch and we will try and make a plan of action,' he said, kissing her forehead.

***

He was still angry when he returned to the mill and forced himself to concentrate on viewing the progress the proud workers were keen to show him. The cottage was complete; the two bedrooms upstairs with lights and sockets, the kitchen had been completely installed and the cottage looked fantastic except for the very empty room that was to become the bathroom. His idea of having his father come to stay was still a couple of weeks away, but Simon was determined to complete the cottage. The finishing was excellent and he praised the workers enthusiastically.

The mill now had a first floor, complete with an oak floor and exposed beams and the upper windows had been fitted. Claude explained that they were waiting for shutters, but they should be in place by the following week. They were waiting for the architect to release more funds and to tell them what was required next. Simon took the opportunity to call him and set up another meeting, careful to arrange the date before he had to return to England.

He was starving by lunchtime and walked to the *Salamandre* with the men to eat. News of the morning's melodrama was the talk of the restaurant and he was uncomfortable with his friend's private life being discussed so openly. Marie stood at the table, loudly berating the absent husband as a snake with the morals of a dog. Henri called back from the kitchen that they would have to find another baker for the restaurant's bread.

Jojo nudged him to pass the wine and with a wink mentioned that with the cottage finished Simon could offer the pretty girl a room. The look Simon gave him silenced him and the others, who suddenly began to concentrate on their lunch. It was just playful boisterousness, but Simon was offended by the insinuation, and the men knew it.

He left early to call round to see how she was, but the *boulangerie* door was locked and her little Citroen was missing from the square. He called his architect and asked to pop in later that afternoon and was squeezed in at the end of the day.

Back at the mill, he took some measurements for a bathroom suite and then drove off to Périgueux to choose fittings and tiles. He found it difficult to concentrate and took longer than really necessary, suddenly doubting himself and his choice, but eventually the decisions were made and he began the detour back to Sarlat to meet the architect.

***

It had always been his intention to reinstate the mill wheel and the workings, but mainly as a heritage option, to preserve the old workings for posterity, and his own curiosity and pleasure, but he now found himself discussing the possibility of small-scale flour production and the installation of a baker's kitchen. As the words came out he watched the architect's eyebrows raise slightly. Simon ignored the silence and babbled on about the possibility of heritage funding and finally stopped about ten minutes later.

'This is *not* what you said you wanted at the beginning of the project', the architect said as tactfully as he could. Simon was aware of sounding like a madman, but pressed on, explaining the possible sale of the existing bakery, and how the mill was an obvious answer to the problem.

'It's an obvious progression, and perhaps it would draw more people to the village as a tourist attraction *and* allow the keeping of the bakery.'

'As far as your plans are concerned there would only be a small change to the ground floor to allow for a commercial kitchen, so we will leave them as they are. I will send you some links to possible heritage funding, and perhaps your *mairie* will be prepared to help with the costs.'

Simon left the office feeling a little better. He'd speak to the *maire* before talking to Émilie, and with a spring in his step he returned to St. Honoré via the leafy countryside, enjoying the warm breeze and feeling rather pleased with himself. Excitement bubbled up in him as he parked outside the mill, and he had to force himself to take one step at a time.

'Pull yourself together mate' he said out loud to himself. 'She's going through hell right now and you don't want to offer her something just to see it fall apart.'

He took a deep breath and decided to visit the *maire* in the morning. This afternoon, late as it was, he'd mention to the contractors that they would be starting on the ground floor of the mill building shortly.

He called them together and explained that now that the staircase was effectively in place, they'd have a look at the stone flagged floor. He'd talk to Philippe, who was a stone mason, to get his expertise on this part of the project and called round to invite him for a beer.

Chapter 9

The *Salamandre* was busy. It was the end of June and there was a mix of tourists and locals eating on the veranda, out on the pavement and inside. The weather was perfect, with swallows wheeling in an azure sky and the temperature conducive to sitting outside in the sun; but because all the tables were taken by tourists he sat at the bar, ordered a large beer and waited for Philippe. As he sat, watching the outside of his glass condensate, he admired his little mill across the road. From the outside it still looked a little the worse for wear, but he knew how much work had been done, and could envision the finished property. The stones were glowing ochre in the evening light, and he watched swallows swooping over the mill pond and the leat, dipping their beaks to have a drink or catching insects. The noisy frogs had quietened down over the last week or so, and the whole scene reminiscent of a Constable painting.

What it needed was a nice new wooden wheel to help the cascade of soothing water, some nice roses outside the door, and perhaps one of those- what had Émilie called it? An Albitzia - to plant for shade outside the cottage. Maybe in a couple of years they could sit and have a nice little supper together under the shade. Who knew what a couple of years would bring for either of them. The future was unclear at the moment, a bit like the still muddy waters under the space where the new wheel would go sometime in the next year or so.

His fanciful daydreaming was interrupted by Philippe pulling the stool next to him and sitting heavily. He'd obviously had a hard day, and Henri was already pouring a large beer for him. He nodded, drunk deeply and put the empty glass down.

'Bon,' he said with a sigh.

Simon signalled Henri to refill the glass, and over the next half hour Simon explained his idea to Philippe in a low voice. He was aware that Jacques was sitting in the back of the bar nursing a glass of red wine, trying to eavesdrop and the last thing he wanted was *anyone*; least of all Jacques, knowing what he was discussing. Philippe listened intently and when Simon had finished his explanation, he sighed and paused for a few minutes before delivering his thoughts.

'My friend, this is an ambitious idea. I understand you wish to help Émilie, but have you *really* considered the implications? Allowing a business to operate from the mill will involve a considerable commitment. Even if you rent the space to her, what if you have a disagreement in future?'

'I've thought of that. Realistically, I intend to renovate the mill to become functional again, so it's the next logical step. If there is to be milling of flour then logically there should also be a baker. I know Émilie enough to know she would be an excellent choice – better than a complete stranger. I think if we could get a little funding then it would work; and despite what people think, I'm *not* a millionaire. I need some funding to carry this off. The village would keep their bakery and she would have both a business and could maybe afford to rent a small place in the village. Will you come with me to speak to the *maire*?'

Philippe considered the facts for a few quiet moments.

'The husband has already advertised the place for sale, but I think it will not sell quickly. Normally, the place would sell complete – a business, but this would mean another baker in the village. Let's speak to the *maire* about your idea.'

They sat quietly drinking their beer for a few moments, before Philippe laid his hand on Simon's wrist, 'You like this woman?' His dark eyes twinkled.

'Yes; but this is *not* a romantic gesture. It's logical.'

'Hmmm. Logical. *Of course.*' Philippe rolled his eyes and laughed. '*D'accord.* We speak to the *maire* tomorrow at lunch. I will invite him.'

Philippe got up, slapped Simon on the shoulder and took his leave, '*Á demain.*'

As he walked home, Philippe was bursting with pride for his new friend. Such a noble gesture. The Englishman was almost thinking like a true Frenchman. He also smiled as he imagined his wife's delight at the gossip, which he would impart in his own good time. However, she may have been right in her prediction of the union of the miller and the baker, he smiled to himself. *L'amour.* Who can resist?

***

Simon returned to the mill cottage and prepared a small chicken salad together with a supermarket baguette. The bread was of course a disappointment compared to his normal fare, but he chewed and washed it down with some red wine as he sat outside the cottage. The heat had, as usual increased since lunchtime and was expected to hover around 15 degrees through the night. He watched the hoopoo on the lawn, spearing the ground with its curved beak in search of insects, and wondered sadly if Émilie had recovered from her shock that morning.

He reflected on the day's events. France was a country of strong sentiments, where passions simmered under the polite veneer. Just because people didn't talk about their personal triumphs or tragedies, it didn't mean they were less keenly felt. He could only imagine what the girl was going through. With his own divorce still not settled, he could sympathise with the betrayal and hurt; but to face losing not just a marriage, but a home and livelihood all at the same time? No wonder she was heartbroken. Philippe had reassured him that the place would not sell quickly - so they had a little time to prepare. It was such a big decision he'd taken - to offer her business premises at the mill; and he realised and accepted that his feelings for the pretty little baker were more than just casual. He *really* liked her, enjoyed her company and looked forward to seeing her every morning at the bakery and throughout the day. When they had finally gone out for dinner, he'd found her quick-witted, entertaining and pleased that she enjoyed the same things as himself. How would his offer be interpreted? An offer from a foreigner, and almost a stranger. He'd hate to think that she might suspect an ulterior motive. He repeated his comment earlier to Philippe out loud - 'It's logical.'

Who was he trying to kid? Inside; in his heart he admitted he'd fallen for her, but would she even consider his offer? There was no point in trying to second-guess the situation, and no point in worrying over things that he had no control over. He sighed and finished his glass of wine. As dusk fell, and the singing frogs began their song, and the bats began to fly over the *étang*, he smiled and relaxed. Everything will look better in the morning, he told himself firmly, and went to bed.

***

When the workforce arrived the next morning, Simon was already brushing out the ground floor of the mill, creating clouds of gently undulating dust and stoor. He summoned the crew to the *Salamandre* for a meeting over coffee and pastries and explained the plan of attack. Without directly mentioning the situation at the *boulangerie* he told the men that they must divide into two parties - one group to press on with refurbishing the ground floor of the mill. The second, smaller group were to finish the bathroom in the cottage, and then join the others. They were to begin immediately with Jojo to liaise direct with the architect or himself, and to give him details of the supplies they needed. Everything else could wait. The first huge job was the lifting, levelling and sealing of the flagstones on the ground floor. Then they would await revised plans from the architect. Eyebrows lifted around the table, and although the curiosity of the men was almost palpable, they just quietly nodded their acceptance. He'd caught the mood and looked at them seriously.

'I can't tell you anything else at the moment, but the project must be adjusted *and* accelerated, so let's get going. *Allez.*'

Whilst the men returned to the mill under Jojo's command, Simon walked round to the *boulangerie*. He could see Émilie serving behind the counter and she was pale with dark smudges under her eyes. His heart sank to see her suffering; but with a crowd of villagers in there trying to elicit information from her regarding the previous day's juicy events and who'd be eavesdropping any and all conversation between the two of them, he decided to call back later. No point in feeding the fire, he thought. Instead, he turned round and headed back to the mill, where at least he could do something useful until the lunch meeting with Philippe and the *maire*.

***

The work was hot and dirty, but when he finally managed to grab a quick shower just twenty minutes before twelve, he felt happier in himself. He pulled a clean tee shirt and jeans onto his still damp body and headed to the bar. Philippe waved and he saw that the *maire* was already seated and the wine; a large carafe of chilled rosé, he noted, was on the table.

They shook hands and Philippe took charge of the conversation; half in English and half in French. The *maire* seemed pensive at first, unsure as to the purpose of the meeting, but Philippe quickly and quietly explained the idea, and as the wine disappeared from the carafe, he settled with nods and smiles. Philippe explained the many advantages of the proposed expansion of the mill project to include a traditional *boulangerie;* and the *maire* who was not a stupid man, could visualise the increased taxes coming from the proposed business, the hordes of families visiting an attractive addition to the village and the additional revenue for the bar, restaurant and other businesses in the village. And then there was the elevation of the status of the village to *heritage site* and the additional funding that went along with this.

He began to smile whilst making notes, and having finished a delicious meal of baked camembert with pears, he stood up from the table. He grasped Simon's hand firmly and said, 'I will attend to the necessary. Get your architect to message me,' and suddenly left. Simon was in a state of dismay, but Philippe poured him another glass of rosé, and indicated it was all fine.

'We'll need to talk with Émilie now,' Simon began, 'to see how she feels about…'

He stopped in mid-sentence as he became aware of a familiar and *very* unwelcome voice. 'Oh God, what is *she* doing back here again,' he groaned, and quickly made excuses to leave, telling Philippe to tell Henri he'd settle the bill in the evening. He nipped down the stairs to the street as quickly and quietly as he could and almost ran around the corner.

Hoping, rather than believing he'd got away with it, he assessed his options. He couldn't go back to the mill; she'd surely see him; so he quickly walked into the empty *boulangerie*. There was no sign of Émilie, who must be in the bakery kitchen, but he could certainly hear the clip clop of Jenn's towering high heels following quickly, so he darted upstairs.

He heard the door being flung open and could hear Jenn's nasally, strident voice,

'Simon? *Simon!* I know you're in here Simon! I saw you run around the corner…'

At the same time, he heard a very angry Émilie coming out of the bakery kitchen and demanding to know what was happening.

'What are you shouting about? There is no-one here but me and I'm *closed*! Please leave!'

'You're *hiding* him!' shrieked Jenn, 'I should have guessed there was *something* going on between you two…'

From his position upstairs he couldn't actually see what

was happening, but realised what an unfortunate position he'd put that poor girl in. He sat on the bed, listening intently to the ruckus downstairs. 'Noo!...You can't go in there! Get out!' Émilie squealed angrily. Jenn must have barged into the kitchen, he thought. A moment later (with his heart pounding at the sound of a scuffle downstairs) he heard Émilie order the intruder out of the shop, 'I told you no-one was here, now get OUT!'

Eloise, roused by the commotion and her mistress's raised and angry voice began to bark loudly and continuously. Simon, helpless and useless, rolled his eyes - it was just like some old TV soap opera.

Finally the door banged and Émilie was swearing and cursing in garbled; and thankfully unrecognisable French. He could still hear Jenn babbling loudly outside in very broken French; God knows who to. The silly girl was incredibly loud and embarrassingly *English*. Any villagers roused by the commotion wouldn't have a clue what was going on, but would undoubtedly put two and two together and make five.

He needed to return downstairs and explain sheepishly to Émilie why he was in her bedroom and stood up and was about to leave the room when he heard feet pounding quickly up the stairs.

Not knowing who was approaching the room in such a hurry, he furtively glanced round the room. Hiding now and explaining later was a good choice. Under the bed was impossible for his large frame, but the wardrobe; an old and huge walnut *armoire* appeared to be the only option.

'Jesus!' he said, opening the door and clambering in amongst the cramped clothes. Although large in a small bedroom the *armoire* was not built to contain large, well-built men. He held the door shut with a finger, unable to close the damn thing from inside, and held his breath. 'I'm hiding in a wardrobe,' he thought to himself. If this got out, he'd never live it down, he thought as the absurdity of his situation dawned on him, as he waited, heart hammering, praying that he wouldn't be discovered.

***

Suddenly, Émilie wrenched open the door, her eyes opening wide with shock, but instead of shouting at him she pushed him deeper inside and climbed in besides him! The bottom of the sturdy *armoire* creaked with the sudden weight and Simon was pushed against the back panel as Émilie wriggled against him and grabbed the inside of the edge of the door to close over the door. Her eyes met his and he opened his mouth to blurt out some stupid explanation, but she firmly put her hand over his mouth, shook her head and mouthed the word, 'Husband!' and sure enough another voice downstairs, insistent and angry called up,

'Émilie! *Où es-tu?*'

Silence in the cramped wardrobe. Simon inhaled the delicate scent of vanilla from her hair as she pushed herself further against him.

'Émilie!' The voice was getting angry; and louder. *And nearer*. Simon could hear him taking the stairs two at a time, and could feel the girl cowering next to him; but he daren't move lest the door fly open. Finding the two of them in such a situation *would* give him ammunition for the divorce and also plenty of unwanted gossip for the village.

Suddenly there were *more* voices downstairs, including Josiane Cholet arguing with 'the husband' and telling him if he didn't leave immediately, she would call the *gendarmes*. Jenn was obviously still outside, barking something loudly in Franglais that nobody could understand. Josiane was now shouting to attract attention outside the shop which seemed to have the desired effect.

The heavy footsteps stopped abruptly and then thumped back downstairs. Josiane continued to harangue and scold the intruder. Éloise was barking *and* growling and the husband must have finally given up because there was a tremendous bang of the front door, which shook the bell and the doorframe, and then the disturbance carried on for a few moments outside.

Finally the voices became quieter and Simon and Émilie, still cramped inside the wardrobe heard an expensive car screech off, followed quickly by the clip-clopping of high heels marching away. Émilie put a finger on his lips whilst they waited; straining to hear.

In the deafening silence that ensued, the pair of fugitives, hardly daring to breathe for a few seconds slowly pushed open the wardrobe door. Émilie stepped out first, followed by Simon, gulping air and stretching after the imprisonment. They turned to each other sheepishly and began to giggle at the absurdity of the situation, releasing the tension of the past few minutes. Then the girl took a deep breath and flung herself into his arms unexpectedly and the two fell onto the bed together, laughing. He covered her face with kisses, murmured her name and tried incoherently to explain why he'd been hiding; but she smiled that irritatingly bewitching smile and instead he found himself kissing her; and to his surprise and delight she was kissing him back.

***

Josiane Cholet, the heroine of the hour; sent the slowly emerging villagers back to their homes, explaining that the disturbance was a domestic incident and now finished. After a few minutes with the square once again quiet and the swallows twittering the only noise, she returned to her house, closed the door behind her and helped herself to a small nip of *eau de vie* from the cupboard. Then settling herself at the kitchen window she waited and watched; and watched and waited, and when no-one appeared to leave the *boulangerie*, she began to smile to herself and hum; and was still humming when her husband appeared an hour later from work.

She linked her arm in his and suggested with a smile that they head to the bar for an *aperitif*. Philippe raised his eyebrows, but washed and changed dutifully whilst she prepared some tapas for their supper, humming an old folk song quietly as she popped a bottle of *crémant* in the fridge to chill for a while. Her eyes were full of excitement and mischief, which he could not fail to notice. She must have some news or gossip to share with him; and why not, over a pre-dinner drink. He might even tell her his *own* gossip. She kissed him lightly on the cheek and slipped her hand in his, and together they walked past the *boulangerie* towards the bar, possibly just hearing a whisper of a giggle from the room above the bakery as they walked past.

Chapter 10

The morning of the Fête de la Saint Jean dawned with a clear azure sky, and the *maire* was delighted. He flung open the curtains of his bedroom, opened the window and threw open the shutters to better view the blue sky and sunshine. From this window he could see that tables were already set out in the square outside the church and soon he would be marshalling his volunteers and food stall-holders to create the large outdoor restaurant for the big day. Already from his modest house at the top end of the village he could hear the sound system for the band being set-up. He rose from his bed and nudged his plump wife Nicole.

'Two more minutes,' she murmured and pulled the sheet over her head. He slapped her rump affectionately and headed for the shower. When he emerged, she had left the bed and could be heard downstairs, cooking; he could smell a delicious omelette with…*cèpes* and bacon. He sniffed appreciatively and walked quietly downstairs to the kitchen.

Nicole had a large pot of coffee and some fresh bread already on the table, and he sat awaiting the arrival of the omelette, which filled the plate. He was very lucky indeed to have such a wonderful cook as a wife, he thought to himself as he took the fork and dug into the billowing softness. The first mouthful was always the best. A feast for the eyes and the tongue he sighed, and forced himself to eat slowly.

'Émilie was looking very pleased with herself this morning,' Nicole mentioned as she poured him a large bowl of coffee.

Georges grunted. The Englishman must have told the baker

of his idea, he thought, pulling the fresh baguette apart with his hands. The proposition would solve a big problem for her *and* bring a big advantage to the village. He had heard the village tittle-tattle of a romantic liaison beginning to blossom between them and was pleased for them both. He had money and she was a beauty; although a little too skinny for Georges personal taste; he liked women to be curvy and full; like Nicole - a peach in full bloom.

His daughter appeared, kissed him on his head, sat beside him, reading the messages on her mobile phone and oblivious to everything else.

They ate quietly. The bells from the church rang out seven o'clock and the *maire* began to shovel omelette and bread into his mouth as quickly as possible. Nicole refilled his bowl with more coffee and sat down beside him.

'I'll come over around nine and help you set out the chairs,' she murmured.

'The Englishman is planning to start milling flour again when the mill is complete' he confided conversationally.

'Well, that makes sense, and maybe Émilie Fournier will be able to use the flour…*if* she still has a bakery to run,' his wife commented with a sad shake of her head. 'That husband of hers is a snake! Leaving her a year ago to run the business herself; not that he actually *worked* when he was here; and now returning to divorce her, sell up and ruin her life again!'

He met her eyes and tapped his nose, not divulging the bigger secret that he knew. Georges knew how to keep a secret. It was necessary in his position; and after all, nothing was settled until it was settled correctly and on paper. Today it was not possible to forward the momentous plan of the mill, he was far too busy with the fête, but perhaps by the end of the week things would be moving forward. Nicole could *surely* wait a few more days before winkling the secret out of him; unless his beautiful peach of a wife would manage to tempt him and tease it out from him later that night; it being the fête after all.

He sighed with delight at the thought until he realised she was watching him intently.

Nicole could see the wheels in her husband's head turning, and knew he had a secret. Of course she was itching to know, but she would make him tell her later, when they were alone and he wasn't thinking about the fête, so she smiled and passed him a flaky croissant.

'Are you coming home for lunch?' she asked as he popped the whole thing into his mouth and picked up his keys.

'Of course my little peach!' he kissed her roughly on the cheek; and with a smile and a contented belly, left to begin supervising the plans for the festival.

***

At the mill Jojo and his team were using scaffolding poles and wooden wedges to correct the sunken floor. Simon had arrived after the men and there were a few smiles and nudges as he changed from last night's clean clothes back into workwear.

'Can't a man have any privacy?' he grinned back at them and began to help them move some flagstones.

The morning passed quickly and at eleven the architect arrived to take some measurements, blustering that he was incredibly busy and that on this day it was a huge inconvenience. Considering he was being paid a large sum of money already, Simon and the men ignored him and let him get on with a rapid tour of the ground floor. At ten minutes to twelve he beckoned Simon to him and a hurried conversation assured Simon that the changes downstairs would in fact be minimal - after all the building was already a mill and there was plenty of room for both a commercial kitchen and even a small shop and storage at the side.

'I'll work on the amended drawings tomorrow. My wife is insisting we take the children to the Fête at Saint Leon sur Vezere where we live.' He rolled his eyes with a sigh and shook Simon's hand before leaving.

***

Over lunch at the *Salamandre* the men were joking and planning their evening. The fête was the big event of the year in the village and everyone would be there. Simon had agreed that they could all leave early and turn up a little later in the morning. He explained that there was nothing like it in the UK; but Jojo, the font of local knowledge mentioned Midsummer's Eve. 'It must have been a similar thing, with a feast and a large fire. You English have just neglected your heritage. But now, you are here in France and will enjoy the feast here and the fire afterwards. And, I hear Georges has organised a firework display also.'

Simon stuffed slices of roast duck and *cabécou* into his mouth. He was starving and his hurried departure earlier that morning from Émilie's bed without breakfast was making his stomach growl. He nodded, washing down the sweet duck and salty goat's cheese with some rosé.

'Of course,' Jojo added, with a wink to the others, 'You know that the feast of Saint John is a pagan fertility festival? Oh yes, it is the time for feasting and dance and love.'

The men sniggered and Claude, waving his fork, and addressing a captive audience added, 'Yes, there are many babies born exactly nine months after the feast. It is true! I myself have *two* March children,' he grinned, and Jojo slapped his back. 'You old goat!'

'And the band tonight are very good; they do some traditional dances for the old people and then later in the evening, some pop tunes.'

Marie appeared to remove their dirty plates. 'When's your birthday Marie?' Jojo asked, with mock innocence.

'End of March. Why; are you going to give me an early gift, *un petit cadeau*?' she flirted outrageously and fluttered her eyelashes, grinning till the dimples in her cheeks deepened.

They laughed together; she'd been eavesdropping the

101

conversation obviously. Some other diners turned to catch the risqué conversation and laughter, and Simon's eye was drawn to the rear of the bar, where Jacques was scowling with his glass of *vin rouge*. Marie saw where his attention was focused and shrugged, 'He has promised to behave; *haven't you Jacques?*'

The old man banged his empty glass down and walked out muttering. Marie shrugged, 'We'll see how long his good behaviour lasts,' she said ominously, her good humour gone, '*Chassez le naturel, il revient au gallop.*'

Simon looked at her quizzically for an explanation.

'A leopard does not change his spots' she said primly and took away the plates without explaining what she meant by this curious statement.

Music began to emanate from the square and the men took this as the signal to return to work. Simon followed them back and only once cast his eyes longingly towards the *boulangerie*. Émilie was putting up some bunting on the shop front and playfully blew him a kiss. Jojo, ever watchful saw the exchange and nudged Simon.

'That is a beautiful girl, my friend; and she likes you. Perhaps you need to ask her to dance tonight. A man can be very lonely without a good woman, and *she* is a good woman. I'm sure you could make each other happy.'

Simon pushed Jojo's shoulder playfully, 'Ah, but I am not as practiced in the ways of romance as you French are!' he laughed.

'This is true. The Frenchman is of course, the best lover in the world. Perhaps a little of the French luck in love will rub off on you. You can only offer her your heart tonight and see what happens.' Jojo's eyes twinkled and then he gruffly proclaimed he had dust in his eyes and walked purposely back to his tools.

'*Allez!*' he called to the men, 'Let's work hard and then tonight enjoy our evening!'

*****

They downed tools an hour later and began to drift off. Simon inspected the bathroom next to his bedroom. The shower and bath had been installed and the tiling was on the walls but not yet grouted. Claude had complained that they could not do *everything* in a day - the tiles needed to be left to settle. But Simon was pleased. The men had worked hard. In the mill the floor was partly reconstructed with lime mortar between the joints on at least three-quarters of the floor. There was a tiny slope away towards the door, just in case there was any further water penetration, but Jojo had raised a doorstep as part of the process and tomorrow or the next day they could think about a proper solid door to be fitted to make the building secure.

***

Émilie called '*Coucou*' from behind him and he turned and swept her into his arms.

'Perfect timing,' he whispered and held her tight. Blushing, she wriggled from his arms, 'People may be looking.'

'So, let them look. I'm not ashamed. Please tell me you don't regret last night?' He looked into her brown eyes, searching for any hesitancy; any regrets, but saw none. She was inscrutable; a mystery, and totally enjoying playing the game of French seduction and romance, whilst he had his heart firmly pinned on his sleeve now.

She pushed him playfully inside the doorway and kissed him, her soft lips lingering on his for just a second.

'So, shall we go to the fête together?' she asked coquettishly, ignoring his question.

'I'd rather take you to bed,' he said kissing her neck.

'Behave yourself!' she giggled. 'We must be prudent and above suspicion. We are both still technically married.'

'Alright, *Ms* Fournier. Shall I call round to collect you, or will just meet, by chance at the fête?'

'At the fête please.'

'Are you going to wear that ridiculously tiny wisp of a

103

dress?' he asked saucily, indicating the almost transparent floral sundress she was wearing.

'What, *this* little thing? I only put it on to see if you were still interested. But I'm going to change into an even more alluring one this evening!' she laughed huskily, and beat a hasty retreat out of the door.

Simon stood and watched her skip up the *chemin*. He was happier than he'd been in a long time. The previous night they had made love and it was sweet and lovely and easy between them, and then afterwards had laughed about the whole wardrobe situation. When at last they lay quietly, holding each other with Simon kissing the thick brown curls that cascaded down her tanned shoulders, he decided it was the right time to tell her about his plans for the mill and how he could offer her a secure workplace. She listened intently, waiting until he'd quietly explained the whole idea, about moving everything - the fittings, equipment and supplies into the ground floor of the mill. Of course, they were not quite ready; he murmured, but that the *maire* and Philippe had mentioned that the building she was currently in would not sell immediately. He and the workmen would concentrate on getting it fitted with water and electricity and anything else she needed. Would it be alright? Would she consider it?

***

To his horror Émilie had begun to quietly cry and he had held her quietly waiting for her sobs to end. He explained gently that it was 'logical'; that he had intended for the mill to be functional, and that it seemed that fate had made everything fall into place at the right time. Teardrops hung on her lashes and he had placed a finger on her lips. 'As far as this romance is concerned', he recalled saying, 'let's just see how it goes.'

She had nodded and kissed his finger. Simon's heart turned over as he recalled how she'd then kissed inside the palm of his hand, her soft lips somehow finding his work-hardened hands sensitive and sensual and how they ended up making love again. The memory of their first night as lovers roused him again and impatiently, he banged the doorframe with his fist and told himself off. 'Simon, old son; you'll never get to see Cinderella at the ball if you keep this up!' he'd said and strode outside for a much-needed cold shower.

***

Jacques was watching him from his weed-infested yard. The midsummer heat and evening showers had encouraged the weeds to grow waist-high and the cottage had almost disappeared under a blanket of green. You couldn't really call it a garden. Even if you were a rewilding fanatic, the piles of old broken slates and pieces of discarded guttering, although providing homes for some of the creeping and slithering creatures just screamed neglect. The old man was suddenly filled with jealousy and hatred. With his stained thumb and forefinger he crushed the stub of a cigarette and tossed it aside angrily.

So, now they were actually working on the floor of the old mill! Soon the little pot of gold, *his* little pot of gold would be discovered! It must be somewhere hidden in the floor or the old walls.

He had been watching them this morning, and the urgency with which the workmen had transferred their work from the cottage and the upstairs of the mill to the ground floor puzzled him; there was a story there that he was not party to, but now he was definitely running out of time. He'd overheard snatches of conversation at the bar, but not enough to enlighten him and as he was still being shunned by most of the village couldn't very well ask anyone. His anger simmered as he felt the whole village was against him, and it was all the fault of this interloper. *Everything* was his fault!

***

Today; St John's Eve, was busy with visitors and families enjoying themselves. Cars flooded into the village and the car park was full, with many cars parking at the side of the road opposite the *Salamandre* and down even to outside the *chemin* of his cottage. He'd put out a selection of his paintings for sale, hoping to tempt the visitors, but no-one was interested; not even in the nudes and landscapes he'd knocked off. His earnings were not sufficient to keep him in the style he wanted and the enticement; the shapeless, indefinite, but oh-so felicitous probability of the stash of gold was the main thing that filled his head; apart from revenge on the Englishman. What right did this foreigner; this upstart have, buying the *moulin* and all it contained! It wasn't right! And now he appeared to be in some sort of romance with that baker woman. Worming his way into the heart of the community, whilst he; born and bred in the village was shunned and gossiped about. He seethed with jealousy; allowing the green-eyed monster to run rampant in his head. And today, the big day for the village, the Englishman would be at the fête as if he'd always been part of the community. Sitting with friends, dancing with a pretty girl and eating like a king! It just wasn't *fair*!

He himself would attend, of course. Someone would leave some unfinished bottle of wine on a table, which he'd casually lift and make his own, and wander round the food stalls. Not for him the expensive steak-frites or *confit de canard*; but possibly he could order a half a pizza; his savings would stretch to that. He spat in the general direction of a struggling hawthorn sapling and watched as his spittle slithered and then fell onto a glistening greyish mushroom. Maybe he could pick a few of the field mushrooms, the *rosé des prés*, and add them to a slice of pizza to make it tastier.

***

'*Mon Dieu*!' he cried, slapping his forehead and almost knocking out the evil idea that had manifested itself suddenly in his head. That was the answer! If Simon Parker, the English *voleur* was intent on stealing the gold of old Renauld; the gold that was meant for Jacques, then a few choice specimens of *le calice de la mort* or Death Cap mushroom on his pizza would deal with him. In the general mêlée of the crowd, dancing and noise, no-one would notice Jacques substituting his own plate, with a slice of doctored pizza for the plate of the Englishman. Immediately overjoyed at the simplicity and surety of his idea he rummaged round his shack, found a knife & basket and donned a pair of surgical gloves. Lighting a final celebratory cigarette he then made his way quietly into the woods to hunt for a few of the fatal mushrooms. Even if it took him the rest of the day he'd find a couple of fat specimens. What could possibly go wrong?

Chapter 11

Simon had an hour to kill before heading over to the fête. The men had left and he was impatient to go and see Émilie, and of course, experience his first ever fête. He tidied the kitchen and put a bottle of white wine in the fridge, in case she agreed to come back and stay at his cottage; although he felt she would surely refuse. She perhaps felt the romance was moving too fast, and he would not risk chasing her away. This sweet and slowly developing romance was so different from his intense relationship with Jenn.

He squirmed slightly at the memory of their initial meeting at a party, where they were both a little drunk. He'd been dazzled by her good looks and flirtatious manner. They'd been introduced by the host of the party; a well-to-do businessman with a young trophy wife and a mortgaged-to-the-hilt town house in one of the upmarket areas of Bristol. He should have realised then what sort of woman she would be and shook the memory from his head. At least that disaster was close to finally closing.

Émilie was like a breath of fresh air; sensible, funny, kind and hard-working. Oh; and very, very pretty. He smiled to himself; it wouldn't hurt to make the bed up nicely, and he set to it, plumping the fat new pillows up and lifting his dirty work clothes and popping them in the washing machine. The clock on the living room wall sluggishly announced that it was only quarter to the hour, so he called his dad and was delighted to hear that he was getting ready to go see some of his pals and, *yes*, he was taking his medicine, and *yes*, he was eating.

The busybody from next door (Simon immediately recognised Sally in this description) was insisting on coming round and cleaning too. *Cleaning!*

'You'd think I lived in a midden!' Andrew Parker spat indignantly.

Simon smiled and changed the subject, 'I've met a girl', he said.

'Oh a *girl*! Well, I haven't seen hide nor hair of your *wife*, I must say. You must have told her not to come here anymore, I assume. Can't be long now till your divorce comes through now, eh?' Simon winced at the nasty comment, totally unlike the father he knew. *Had* known, he sadly reflected.

'No, not long now,' Simon agreed; wishing he'd never mentioned the girl. His father had made it sound tainted and casual, and he pushed the negativity away. 'Anyway, I'm off out tonight myself, so let's hope we both have a lovely time. Who are you meeting then?'

'Ted's picking me up. We're off to the bowling club for dinner, and …oh, I'm going to be late if I don't go get changed… Look, have a nice time with your girl. What's her name?'

'Émilie. She's French.'

'Emily. I'll try to remember…Okay son, I'll speak to you soon.'

Simon heard the click of the phone going down at the other end and smiled. Well, things seemed to be going okay at his end, he thought, and decided that he too had better freshen up. They'd eat at the fête, Émilie had suggested; and he was starving. Starving and excited. He stood in his bedroom, staring at the mirror; could he really be so lucky? A beautiful house in a beautiful country and a beautiful girlfriend too? Well, it was early days, but he hoped that she thought of herself as a girlfriend. Tonight he'd make his feelings clear. He grinned at the mirror; 'You old dog!' he told himself and walked outside to the shower.

***

The music had started in earnest and the square was thronged with people, some of the older couples dancing to the traditional tunes the band pumped out. Simon scanned the crowd to see if he could see her. Amidst the sea of colour, scents and noise it was hard to pick anyone out. The band began to thump out an old Johnny Halliday classic and more people suddenly got up to gyrate on the cobbles of the square outside the church. Rows and rows of long tables and chairs had been pulled out of the school, the *salle de fête* and possibly from the neighbouring village to cater for the huge influx of visitors. The heat shimmered in the enclosed square of ochre stone buildings and sweat began to trickle down his back as he crossed back and forth, trying to avoid being bumped by some of the more adventurous dancers.

Stupidly, they hadn't actually chosen a *rendezvous*, so Simon walked past the food stalls over and over. This was torture to a man who'd worked hard all morning and hadn't eaten since lunch. There was a paella stall with an enormous metal pan full of seafood, rice and chicken pieces and the smell of saffron rice, spices and prawns filling the air made Simon's mouth salivate. Next to this, with a huge queue was the barbeque chicken and pork man, who was sweating profusely as he tried to serve as quickly as the customers shouted orders to him. Then the pizza man; making pizzas in a mobile wood-fired oven, and of course, the *tartiflette* stall, with two massive pots full of the aromatic creamed potato, reblochon cheese and some lardons. If he didn't find her soon, Simon was going to give in and grab a plate of something.

And then suddenly the crowd parted and she was standing smiling at him. She was wearing a black *broderie anglais* dress that came to her knees and her hair was caught up in a black hairband, and she was smiling at him. She was simply the most stunning girl Simon thought he'd ever seen, and his heart began to beat like he'd run a hundred metres as he stepped forward towards her.

'I have space at a table with Josiane and Philippe,' she smiled.

'You look amazing,' he said simply, kissing her on both cheeks.

Émilie acknowledged his compliment with a shy smile and took his hand to lead him to the table. She could lead me to the ends of the world and I'd follow her he thought, twining his fingers in her.

Josiane nudged her husband, 'Look. They are in love,' she giggled.

'Pass me that wine, you goose,' Philippe said, 'and leave them alone.'

He poured two glasses of chilled rosé, and beckoned Simon to sit with him.

'Your first fête de la Saint Jean. May you enjoy many, many more.'

Suddenly overcome with gratitude, happiness and love, Simon hugged the man; his friend. Philippe kissed him on both cheeks and pushed him into a chair with a throat clearing cough.

'Now, now! I am going to dance with my beautiful wife before the music becomes too fast' he said gruffly, pulling Josiane out of her chair. Émilie laughed as Josiane clucked indignantly, but allowed herself to be led to the middle of the dancing crowd.

'You are a soft old fool' Josiane said, kissing her husband softly on the lips.

'Be quiet and stop leading; or I'll stand on your toes,' he answered, pulling her closer into his arms. They danced round and round a few times before rejoining the couple on the long bench table.

Simon was looking at the huge crowd of people filling the tables in the square in wonder, 'I never knew the village had so many inhabitants.'

'Oh people come from all over. This is a big event in the village calendar. Do you want to go and choose something to eat?' Émilie asked, sipping the cool wine.

'No, I just want to look at you right now. Have you thought about my offer?'

'Yes, but I want to make sure you understand my position,' she answered very seriously. 'We need to draw up an official contract, where I will rent the ground floor from you. Just in case there are any misunderstandings later. Not that I think there will be,' she added hastily, 'but Simon; it's such a big thing you do, to offer me to have my business. Are you sure?'

He nodded and took her hand, leading her to dance, now that the band was playing a slightly slower number. He placed his hand about her waist and with his other hand held her fingers tightly. Her scent; that fresh yet musky vanilla was all around her hair and he lowered his head closer to hers. 'I'll contact my French solicitor and get something drawn up after the weekend', he murmured. 'God, you smell good enough to eat!'

'Well, if monsieur is *that* hungry, we will visit the stalls and satisfy you!' she said laughing, pulling him towards the food stalls.

He just managed to whisper in her ear, 'I'm hungry for *you*, you little minx!' but she just laughed and insisted that he choose something.

'Pizza!' he declared loudly, whilst Émilie decided on the paella. 'I'll meet you back at the table' he called to her.

As they both joined separate queues for food, and oblivious to everything and everyone around them, Jacques smiled from the shadow of the old school door. He had correctly guessed he would choose pizza; he was *always* eating pizza, the fool! He was standing smoking and stroking his moustache. He'd followed Simon from a distance and was watching the couple, who only had eyes for each other.

'L'amour!' he spat crossly, and drew the disgusted attention of a family sitting on the nearby wall eating fries. He moved towards the crowd, always keeping far enough away not to be seen, but near enough to watch the couple. He'd dressed for the event in his least dirty trousers and old tee-shirt; after all - he wanted to blend in. He had his little plastic bag with his bottle of wine and the innocuous silver foil package inside. He'd cooked the three deadly specimens and cut them into small pieces, ready to deploy onto the Englishman's pizza, although with small pieces it would have been just as easy to secrete them into whatever he'd decided to buy. So small as not to attract attention, but even the smallest pieces once eaten would be fatal.

With his mad excitement mounting, his hands were sweating. He needed a drink, and prided himself for having the sense to also bring a half-drunk bottle of red wine to still his nerves and conscience. No paying inflated prices to the wine sellers here! So he sat at the edge of the crowd, took a swig from the bottle and watched the couple sit down at one end of a crowded long table. The Cholet's were next to them, but Jacques knew Philippe would not stay late. Next to them were an English couple. He didn't know their names, but they'd lived just outside the village for a few years. He just had to sit and bide his time. Soon the crowds would thin a little; people would be drunk and not as observant…

He lit another cigarette and waited.

***

Simon and Émilie ate and drank and chatted and danced. Soon the band took a break and the murmur of happy conversation filled the square. Children were laughing and running around, and Georges the *maire*; happy to have no threat of rain or thunder was visiting all the tables in turn; chatting and joking, and drinking with mock reluctance many proffered glasses of wine. As the clock in the church tower struck half past nine, Philippe nudged his wife. He was up at six and it was time to leave the festivities. She complained loudly that she wished to see the fireworks and he gently reminded her that *every* year they saw the fireworks; and he wanted an early night.

'Besides,' he said in a whisper, 'we need to leave the love-birds to have some time on their own.'

Josiane's little mouth made an O shape as she understood and she got up immediately, kissed both Simon and Émilie on both cheeks and bid them a '*bon soirée*,' and taking her husband's hand they walked the few yards to their house. 'I'll give you fireworks, you silly goose,' Philippe said, pinching her bottom and pushing her giggling inside the house.

*****

'He's never going to get any sleep with all this noise,' Simon remarked, shaking his head as the band started up again.

'Who said they were going to sleep?' his companion laughed. 'All the Cholet children are born at the end of March.'

Simon laughed, and pulled her onto the dance floor as the band resumed playing some romantic slow tunes. The cobbled dance floor filled with people getting up to dance.

Jacques stretched from his viewing point on the wall. *This* was the moment. Time for him to act. It was so *easy*. The paper plate where the Englishman was sitting had two more slices of pizza remaining. He looked at the rest of the table. The English couple were on their second bottle of red wine and would notice *nothing*. Many others were gathering up their belongings and children and going home. He impatiently opened a new packet of cigarettes. Another minute would make no difference. He pulled the cork from the wine bottle and took another swig, to the disgust of a woman herding her children past the filthy old man. Drinking from a bottle and did you *see* the amount of cigarette ends surrounding him? He overheard her say to her husband, as they scurried past. He didn't care. He never cared what people said about him. Soon he'd be the one laughing.

114

Jacques made his way slowly towards the table. The couple; with eyes only for each other were dancing together, surrounded by other couples. Their end of the table was empty; the other English couple were also dancing, rather drunkenly. Jacques sat down at the table, looked around him furtively to assure himself that no-one was looking, and began to open the small silver foiled package. He carefully removed four pieces of the contents. No chance of donning gloves with so many people still around. He must be careful. With his beady eyes covertly looking around him, he placed the deadly pieces on the two remaining slices of pizza on the paper plate, pushing them into the topping with bare fingers. The tune was only about half-way through, the dancers still engrossed. So far so good. After a few seconds he quietly vacated the chair. The deed was done. With sweating hands he headed to the public toilet and washed and washed his hands. Then he washed them again, drying them on the paper towels and pushing the soiled paper into the bin. He almost included the plastic bag with the remains of the mushrooms, but common sense and fear stopped him. Not here.

He walked back to the food stalls and pushed the plastic bag with its now empty foil package into the large bin almost overflowing with paper plates and plastic cups. Better. He had delivered the deadly instrument of his deliverance. The acid in his stomach rebelled and he decided to return home. He didn't have to stay; didn't have to watch. The mushrooms would do their job. He was filled with a maniacal delight in how *easy* it had all been. He ran a sweaty hand over his forehead and then recoiled. Must go home and wash properly; the last thing he wanted was any trace of the toxin on himself. He turned and walked away, passing the *boulangerie*, the *moulin* and arrived at his own dark house.

A feverish and thorough scrubbing of his hands and face

ensued, with soap and then disinfectant. Then unable to rest, he took up a third packet of cigarettes and began to smoke, sitting outside his door, listening to the last snatches of the band in the heavy, still air.

The fireworks began shortly afterwards and having drunk the last of the *eau de vie* he had in the house, the twisted old man finally fell asleep in his grubby chair, with shadows gathering round him, disturbing his gleeful celebration of the expected and final extinction of his problem. Sleep eventually came but his demons took great delight in tormenting him through the small hours with wretched nightmares.

***

The morning after dawned like any other day. The sun rose into the endless blue sky and the workmen arrived at the *moulin* and quietly resumed work on the mill floor. Claude fuelled his work with a couple of trips to the *Salamandre* for strong coffee and gradually sobered up. Simon had returned alone but happy to his cottage very late the previous evening and looked forward to meeting the architect and going over the plans. Émilie would join him later to discuss where the equipment was to be installed.

The previous evening he had discovered that she had in fact previously bought most of the bakery equipment in her own name and that they would not be included in the sale of the property. She had also confided that her solicitor; a female divorcée from Bordeaux was firmly on her side and would deal with the sale and the divorce. She'd been informed that she'd be divorced in between three and six months if her husband agreed to a split in the only joint asset - the building. Thankfully there were no children of the marriage to complicate things further.

He stopped mixing lime mortar for a minute, whilst recalling their parting. He had walked her home after the fireworks and kissed her chastely on the cheek at her door. 'We need to talk about our future very soon' he'd said. 'I don't want people to

116

talk about you or me for that matter. You and I will be free agents soon.'

'Soon,' she agreed, 'but let's see how things work out *mon chéri*. I will come round in the afternoon tomorrow and we will look at the kitchen and storage in the mill. *Bon nuit.* '

***

Simon sighed and returned to mixing the mortar. Claude was waiting impatiently, staring at him and gesticulating for him to hurry up.

Lunch at the *Salamandre* was subdued with little wine being drunk. It seemed they had all had a bit too much the night before. Marie was bustling around cleaning and setting tables, remarking on how good the band was, how much better the fireworks had been this year and coyly remarked on how good Simon's dancing was, considering he was English.

'Ah, it helps if you have a partner who can dance well', he'd retorted with a smile.

Taking the opportunity, he began to tell them men that Émilie would, in due time be relocating her bakery to the mill; and that afternoon, the *maire*, the architect and Émilie herself would all be at the mill to discuss any modifications to the building to allow for this.

After a moments silence, the men smiled and nodded that this was an excellent arrangement. 'After all, what is a mill without a baker,' Jojo commented. 'It makes sense, and gets her out of the awkward situation of having the building sold.'

Waiting for the questions that never followed, Simon was pleased. He knew they were aware of the delicacy of the new romantic situation, but they never asked. That was private, and they respected it. Lunch ended with lots of coffee and they all returned to their work at the mill, and Émilie caused a few smiles, whistles and giggles as she walked down the *chemin* to join them a few minutes after the clock struck two.

117

Chapter 12

The rest of the afternoon consisted of a fast moving and voluble visitation by the architect accompanied by Émilie, who had armed herself with her phone and a clipboard. It began to be clear very quickly that this was to become a battle of wills between the experienced baker and the experienced architect and Simon initially kept out of the way as the earnest and increasingly loud discussion went on in very fast French. The *maire* arrived and with a hushed '*oooh la la*' to Simon they both reluctantly followed the arguing pair in and out of the mill and the attached buildings, with Simon trying and somewhat failing to understand what the architect was getting so worked up about.

Eventually, they agreed to discuss the alterations required calmly and in English. Émilie explained that there needed to be just a few *minor* alterations (the architect rolled his eyes at Simon behind her back), and the cost would be quite small (again, more eye rolling), considering the kitchen must comply with the up-to-date food hygiene rules *and* look attractive and traditional.

She turned to Simon and explained in English that the actual space was perfect, and the storage was good, she just needed more electricity, better lighting and wanted to try and conceal as much as possible the necessary stainless steel commercial kitchen. Not to have his professionalism overshadowed by a *mere* baker, the architect argued the situation from his side. He would have to alter the plans to show the additional conduits and water pipes etc; and a new fosse would now be required.

There would be an increased draw of electricity, and a larger distribution box required and *everything* must be in accordance with both the Heritage department at Périgueux and the food regulations. Simon nodded; he'd already realised the plans for the mill building, the attached stores and outside would have to be altered considerably and instead of all the properties using the small fosse planned, they would need a much larger one. Simon could see the costs spiralling with every word the architect uttered.

Seeing his plan to increase tourism and commerce for the village beginning to wilt under financial pressure, Georges interjected and asked for a comprehensive budget of the work the architect envisioned as he *might* be able to draw down some funds from the Department. Simon smiled weakly; any and all funding possible would be needed to pay for the changes and growth of the project. He was beginning to regret his offer to Émilie.

Of course; Georges casually mentioned; this project would undoubtedly mean the architect would be used again for more *prestigious* historical renovations and therefore, it could only be seen to enhance his reputation. Unless, of course, he felt *unequal* to dealing with the Department and then Georges would try and engage a recommended Departmental architect. The bait worked and the architect, drawing himself up to his full height magnanimously agreed to waive the cost of altering the drawings accordingly.

'Bon!' said Georges, 'Now, we celebrate!' he whistled over to *Le Salamandre*, where Marie was wiping down tables, and loudly ordered a bottle of champagne.

The architect pleading pressure of work begged to be excused and made his apologies, escaping to his car.

As they watched him drive away, Georges took the couple across the road and they sat on the veranda of the restaurant where three champagne flutes awaited them and a bottle of champagne chilled in an ice bucket.

'Now, *before* we drink - a few things,' Georges said in halting English. 'You have agreed to this new alliance, yes?'

Émilie and Simon both nodded and Georges continued, 'So, Émilie will continue for a while in the *boulangerie*, I will stall the sale as much as I can, and *you* my friend will allow me to help you with some of the cost.'

Simon stared at him as the *maire* deftly popped the bottle open with a controlled hand and poured three glasses of sparkling champagne. Georges smiled, his dark eyes twinkling mischievously, and he explained,

'I have a small fund to help develop the village and I *think* I can squeeze some more money from the heritage people who work at Périgueux. The orange; as they say is full of juice, but you need to know how to *squeeze* it to extract the juice, yes? Do *not* sign or pay anything till you have shown me the factures!' he ordered sternly, 'It may be that we need to, shall we say, *creatively reword* any factures.'

Simon was lost for words, but Émilie shyly thanked the *maire* and toasted him.

'*Non*, not my health,' he said; 'but to the *moulin* and the *nouveaux boulangerie!*'

They raised their glasses and drank, and then as quick as a fox, Georges stood and excused himself. '*Excusez-moi*, I must make some phone calls before the end of the afternoon, *mes amies*.'

The couple watched the man almost skip down the stairs in his urgency to return to the office and start the ball rolling.

'Now *that* was an interesting development regarding funding.' said Simon, 'I don't really know what to say. The *maire* is full of surprises.' He raised his glass to the girl sitting opposite him, 'Well, *partner*; looks like this could be the beginning of a beautiful friendship.'

Émilie smiled, '*Santé ma chérie.*' She sipped delicately and took a long hard look at the handsome man sitting opposite. He'd come to her rescue more than once and was kind, thoughtful and fitting well into the community; but oh, *so* naïve in the matters of courting. She had no complaints at all about his performance in the bedroom, she smiled to herself, but she would have to be careful. Careful not to lose him, and yet careful not to let him get carried away as the English did. A love affair was pleasant yes, but she would prefer to have Simon Parker as a more permanent fixture. Love, in France was a game that takes time to develop, a game with complicated rules.

***

Her thoughts were interrupted by the wail of a siren, followed by a speeding ambulance hurtling along the narrow road past the *Salamandre* and into the village.

Such occurrences were rare and unsettling and she met Simon's inquiring eyes,

'Probably a road accident or perhaps an elderly person. I will hear in the morning. All news comes to the *boulangerie*.'

The siren faded away into the distance, and they returned to their champagne and each other.

'What are you doing this afternoon?' Simon said finishing his glass of champagne.

'I have nothing planned. Perhaps we can take a more leisurely look about the mill and I will try and explain what I think will be a good layout?'

They thanked Marie as they left and walked across the road towards the mill. Simon collected his mail from the box at the top of the *chemin*. There was just a single, thin envelope from his solicitor in Bristol. He sighed and hoped that this wasn't yet another demand from Jenn. He slit it open with his thumbnail and quickly scanned the contents. Émilie put her hand on his arm, 'Not a problem, I hope?'

'No, it's good news, for once. Since her last surprise appearance, Jenn has decided to accept my terms and has finally signed the divorce papers. Now, I just have to wait.'

She sighed, 'At least it is ending without more anger. There

121

is a French proverb that says *marriages sealed with rings end with drawn knives*.'

He wanted to take this new relationship with Émilie slowly, and didn't want to jinx it by looking too far ahead, or rushing his fences; so avoiding any talk about marriage would have been sensible, but he refused to believe that all marriages were doomed.

He took her hand and kissed her cheek, 'Yes, my marriage has, and perhaps yours too; but not *all* marriages are failures. Enough of the past - come on; let's plan this kitchen-come-shop of yours.'

They walked back to the building, and she tried to explain what she wanted; where and why, and slowly, he began to understand. Her thinking was perfect - a blend of the old (very visible and traditional) and the new (discreetly hidden).

She would have shelves on one side of the attached storeroom, and her main oven would fit at the rear of the main mill room. That way, she explained, customers could see the mill wheel and machinery working *and* watch her take the bread out of the oven as it was fired. The shop area would have a wooden counter; probably oak and they could have some photographs of the mill, both old and new around the walls. She smiled and her enthusiasm was infectious. He found himself swept along with it, imagining customers crowding in to enjoy the spectacle of bread making. Such a simple and yet traditional thing, and who these days was privileged to see it? Certainly not the holiday-makers who would flock to such an attraction.

***

They walked outside, enjoying the peace and tranquillity. The newly planted trees were covered in fresh green leaves and the mill pond was sparkling, home to dozens of dragonflies flitting about the surface. Simon showed her the progress in the cottage, which just needed the bathroom finished off. The rest of the cottage was almost finished and could wait till the mill project was completed. As he showed her the second bedroom she laughed.

'Josiane Cholet says she will keep her little room for me in case I need it quickly.' Simon roared with laughter, 'Well, good luck with that!' he cried; and she playfully slapped his arm.

Their quiet reverie was interrupted by the return of the siren heading towards St Cyprien, and then the shout of Georges from the main road, '*Allez! Vite, vite*!'

They scrambled up the *chemin* and onto the road to see a red-faced Georges and two *gendarmes*.

'Are you *ill* my friends?' Georges demanded of them both. They exchanged confused looks whilst shaking their heads.

'What has happened? What is going on?' Émilie asked.

'One of our English residents has become very ill and is now on his way to the hospital, but it looks very bad, very serious.'

'Who?' Émilie asked, gripping Simon's hand.

'Barrie Curtis. Barrie and Sue who live at the other end of the village?'

'Oh, yes, I met him at the *salle de fete* after the flood, I think. Nice guy.' Simon mentioned, vaguely recalling the couple.

Georges stared at him hard, 'They were sitting at the same table as you at the fête last night.'

'Yes, that's right. When we left Barrie asked me if he could have the two slices of pizza I hadn't eaten. I think he was a bit drunk.'

There was an ominous silence before the penny dropped and Simon exclaimed,

'What! That was *Barrie* in the ambulance? What's happened for God's sake?'

Georges put his hand on Simon's arm, and with an embarrassed cough, indicated the two uniformed officers at his side.

'The *gendarmes* need to ask you both some questions. It appears that Monsieur Curtis has been poisoned.'

Émilie clapped her hand to her mouth in shock. She didn't really know the couple well; they came to the *boulangerie*, of course; but to have a *poisoning* in the village? In *this* village?

'I don't understand,' she said quietly, 'They were fine last night. *We* are fine. Why did you ask if *we* were ill? What did they eat that we…*the pizza*!' she exclaimed as she finally understood.

'We must go to the *mairie* now,' Georges said, pulling Simon's arm, 'Come.'

'Hold on a minute,' Simon said firmly, pulling his arm free. 'I don't understand what is going on here. I had pizza last night, yes, and I'm fine. Barrie asked me if I was going to finish it and I said "No, it's all yours if you want it". Why do the *gendarmes* want *me*?'

The older *gendarme*, whom it now appeared could understand English perfectly, said, 'Because it appears that *your* pizza was the only thing that Monsieur Curtis ate that was different from his wife, and she is well. *Your* pizza appears to have been tampered with. Monsieur Curtis has suspected amanitin poisoning. This is the toxin from the Death Cap mushroom. The hospital will be able to confirm this very soon; he has been severely ill since last night, but his wife did not call the SAMU till this afternoon, because she thought he had just drunk too much. This is a *very* serious matter monsieur. We need to take a statement from you and Madame Fournier here. We have already spoken to Monsieur and Madame Cholet, who were also sitting beside you and the Curtis's.'

Simon and Émilie walked in stunned silence along the road towards the *mairie*, flanked on either side by uniformed *gendarmes*. Whilst Simon was naturally shocked at the news, he was aware exactly how this awful this would look to anyone in the village watching; and from behind closed-over shutters or net curtains they would *certainly* be watching. Talk about a walk of shame, he sighed heavily to himself as he tried to make sense of the sensational details he'd just been told. Georges meantime, was mopping his brow and praying fervently that the sick man would recover. Never; *never* had there been anything like this in this village. In *his* village.

***

The interviews at the *mairie* were eventually concluded after seven o'clock. Émilie had stayed to assist with any translation required, but the older *gendarme* appeared not to need her assistance. He finally put the paperwork away into a folder, and looked at Simon hard.

'I understand this must be difficult for you - a foreign country, a foreign language and an unfortunate incident. I am waiting to hear about the condition of Monsieur Curtis. I believe that you barely knew him, and from what I can see you appear to have no motive to poison this man. Unfortunately we have insufficient information at this time to identify the culprit. I have colleagues going through the food and kitchens of Monsieur Couderc, the pizza man; but there have been no other cases and no evidence of contamination from that source. So, the poisoning begins and ends at the Fête de Saint Jean.'

The policeman continued quietly, testing the point on his sharp pencil against a manicured finger. 'My understanding is that the pizza itself must have been contaminated whilst you were absent from the table. This makes it clear that *either* Monsieur Curtis or *you* were the intended target. I am investigating this time-line of events, but sadly, the physical evidence is no longer available, and I am reliant on witnesses at this time.'

He shifted slightly and sat back in the chair to more easily stare at Simon,

'I also understand from the *maire* that you yourself have had some, shall we say, *problems*, since moving here? Some incidents involving a difficult man in the village?'

Simon sat in silence, trying to keep up with the twists and turns of the policeman's mind. The last two hours had stripped his confidence, torn away his naïve belief that he was now a member of this community, and probably just ruined his love life. He was sitting in a foreign country being questioned as to the possible poisoning of a stranger, and now it seemed that *he* may have been the intended victim? When would he wake up?

'We are interviewing *many* people and there will be an appeal for anyone who saw anything suspicious to come forward. I must look at *all* possible lines of enquiry. Forgive me; I understand that you and Madame Fournier have a - shall we say…friendship?'

At this comment Émilie blushed to the roots of her hair. Simon cringed and dropped his eyes to the floor.

'Perhaps the husband?' the *gendarme* suggested to the girl, who shook her head, '*Non*, he was not there.'

'Ah well, there are some other interesting lines of enquiry I must follow before I uncover the truth of this matter, and of course, more people to interview.'

He tapped the folder on the desk and stood.

'Well, perhaps we shall see each other again?' he mentioned just a shade too casually as he shook Simon's hand; and with a nod to Georges; who shot out of his seat and followed him, he left the building.

***

Simon's emotions were all over the place, with disbelief, sadness, disgust and anger all vying to control him. He took a deep breath to steady his nerves before speaking.

'I don't *believe* it. I don't believe this all just happened. I've just been interviewed about a poisoning and it's possible that I was the *intended* victim? This is like a TV soap! Ever since I arrived here it's been one thing after another. The flooding, then the car brakes… and now someone's been poisoned and the police aren't sure that I wasn't the intended target? Surely we can't blame Jacques for all of this? I've never done *anything* to the man! I just don't *understand* all this. *Why me?*'

'It's an old story. He seems to think; really *believes* that the old owner, Renauld had hidden some gold or money somewhere in the mill. He has said previously that the old man told him this himself. He wanted to buy it when the old man died, but of course, couldn't afford it and had been waiting for the price to drop, and then you came and bought it.'

'So, it's all jealousy? He wants the *mill*? He's tried to kill me to get the mill?'

'No, *chérie* - he wants the money, the *gold*.'

'But there *is* no gold! Good grief, the cottage and now the mill have been torn apart. Trust me, if there *had* been any gold, you and everyone else in the village would have known about it!'

'I know that. We all know that. But we also know that Jacques is a little mad, *un fou furieux,* and a vindictive nasty man, but I can't believe… there must be another explanation', she tried to smile reassuringly, but suddenly his phone began to ring, and before he answered it, Simon turned a grim face to her.

'A man is lying in hospital seriously ill, I've been interviewed in connection with this, but also I could also have been the target. There's *no* evidence and *no* witnesses, and if it was Jacques; well, he's *still out there*.'

He stopped talking abruptly to answer the phone, and then was silent as he listened intently. His perfect life in France; already damaged and unravelling was now completely disintegrating around him.

'I need to leave,' he said simply, standing up. 'My father has had a fall.'

Chapter 13

By driving through the night Simon managed to arrive at the port of Ouistreham, outside Caen on the Normandy coast just seven hours after locking his cottage and leaving the key with Philippe. After sorting his ticket, he waited at the embarkation area impatiently. The ferry would not leave until 0830 and after a quick walk around the port to ease his muscles he tried unsuccessfully to doze in the car.

He'd hurriedly packed an overnight bag and rushed round to the Cholet's to explain very briefly that he'd had an emergency call and had to return to England. Philippe agreed to oversee the workers at the mill, and shook his hand firmly.

'I wish everything to be alright with your father my dear friend. I'm *so* sorry. This, together with everything that has happened here is unfortunate. But, be assured that we will *all of us* look after your home here. Come back soon.'

When Simon had left, he turned to Josiane grimly, 'I hope we *will* see him return soon. I think he needs to be here now to clear his name, and to be *seen* to be clearing it. This could not have happened at a worse time.'

'The man cannot help his father being ill!' Josiane tutted in reply, 'And all this; this …*poisoning* thing must be a mistake!'

Philippe didn't answer, and pulled on his shoes.

'Where are you going?' she asked, casting a look at the clock. It was high time they were both in bed.

'For a walk. I need to clear my head.'

He closed the door behind him with a bang and walked around the corner to the mill, where he sat on the wall facing the *étang*.

The *moulin* and the buildings were in darkness now; and yet still Philippe sat, watching. He asked himself for what? *Why* was he here? He'd had a sense of foreboding since he'd heard the news about the poisoning. That old fool Jacques had really lost it if he'd had anything to do with this. A poisoning! Philippe had known the man since he was a boy. He remembered Jacques father being a drunken bully who beat his wife, until she'd had a beating too many and left, leaving the boy with the father. There had been talk at the time; whether she *had* in fact left the cottage, or whether old Jean had beaten her to death and disposed of the body; why else would she have left the boy? But then a month later, someone had bumped into her in Marseilles, alive and if not happy and well; at least surviving.

Jacques had got in with a bad crowd from one of the larger towns. Drinking led to petty theft, and then one of his so-called friends had named him in a housebreaking that had gone wrong; the householder surprising the lads and them beating him savagely. Jacques had gone to prison for three months and on his return his father; now a wasted alcoholic, had been rushed to hospital with liver failure and died a few days later. With no prospects of legal employment and after his short and educational period in prison sharing a cell with a forger, he had been convinced to try his hand at copying other artists work. Forgery was an *easy* way to make money he'd been told. Sadly, his lack of talent and accuracy meant that he was in no danger of ever being charged with forgery but some of his paintings did actually sell, Philippe reflected with distaste; especially the nudes with almost pornographic poses.

Thief and con-man he may be, but did he have it in him to actually *poison* someone? He wondered. He was convinced that Jacques had been responsible for the flooding at the *moulin*. Such a nasty and vindictive act of closing the *vannes* down, knowing the probable consequences was evil, but it was not an attempt at murder. However, the problem with the brakes on the car; now that *was* getting very near the bone, Philippe thought, and could have resulted not just in one death, but possibly more. The more he thought about it, the more he became convinced that Jacques could indeed take a life.

He sat quietly as the shadows began to gather round him. The single light in the run-down shack downstream from the *moulin* went out. It was a dismal little house, full of sadness and hate. Was there enough hate in the owner to poison someone? Jacques would never openly try something dangerous, Philippe thought; he was always in the shadows, furtive and dangerous, like an adder in the woodpile. There was a saying that poison was a woman's weapon, but Philippe was unsettled and his generous nature was struggling against the realisation that Jacques could indeed be responsible for the poisoning as well as the sabotaged brakes and the flooding incident. It was also clear to Philippe that Jacques had not committed the acts on the spur of the moment, in the heat of anger. Three attempts and none successful; *so far*. This was pre-meditated and that was chilling. To *deliberately* plan to take the life of another was monstrous. Jacques had slipped from hatred and jealousy into the realms of madness. Would the police unearth enough evidence or witnesses to shine the light onto Jacques evil ways? Only time would tell, and they were *frustratingly* slow. Meanwhile, all he could do was keep a watchful eye on the property. At least his friend was out of danger for a while. God knows what would happen when he returned if the police did not successfully conclude their investigation. He resolved to keep a close eye on Jacques too. With a shiver he got off the wall, and trudged back to his house, satisfied that for tonight at least the *moulin* was safe.

***

In Bristol, Simon arrived at the hospital and found Ted and Sally by his father's bed. He'd been put in a small room next to the main ward and was barely recognisable, with tubes and monitors hooked up everywhere. Ted got up stiffly and put his arm round Simon's shoulder, leading him out to the corridor.

'He had a fall on Sunday night, and lay on the floor all night. Sally phoned me in the morning to say she couldn't get in - he'd locked the front door and left the key in the lock. We called the Police and they broke the door in. I'm sorry son, it's not looking good. The doctors have done their rounds, but the staff nurse is around; I'll go find her. You go sit with your dad. He's been unconscious the whole time, but if you hold his hand, he'll know you're there.'

Simon walked back into the small room. Sally looked up and smiled a watery smile with eyes red and swollen. Heavily Simon took the seat next to the bed and held his father's hand. It was cool and suddenly, to Simon's eyes, his once strong father had shrunk before his eyes and looked very old and frail.

There was a huge blue bruise on the left hand side of his dad's face around the eye socket. He couldn't really see its extent because of the oxygen mask, but the beeping of the heart monitor reassured him.

'You alright Sally?' he whispered, and put his arm around the woman who had, since his mother's death become a second mum to him.

She nodded, 'I'm glad you're here love. He's not really opened his eyes, but I think he's comfortable. We found him on the bathroom floor. Must have got up to go to the toilet and taken a dizzy spell or something. Oh - here's the nurse now.'

The nurse beckoned Simon outside and led him to the small office at the back of the nursing station.

'I'm afraid it's not good news, Mr Parker. Your dad appears to have fallen early hours of Monday morning. The neighbour called the police and the ambulance and following some scans we now know he's had a substantial bleed on the brain. We've stabilised him for now, but…' She lifted her tired eyes to meet Simon's gaze. The 'but' was the telling word he realised.

The nurse smiled gently at him, 'He's elderly and the

haemorrhage quite substantial; that together with the damage caused by the fall *and* lying on the floor overnight means the next twenty-four hours will be critical. I understand you've driven from France to get here, I'll need to be able to contact you in the event of any change.'

'Has he been unconscious the whole time? And what's that bruising round his eye?' Simon asked.

'He's not regained consciousness at all. He's also sustained an orbital skull fracture – that's the bruising round the eye, and a femoral neck fracture to the left leg when he fell. That's about an inch or so from the hip joint. We're waiting to see if he stabilises before we'll consider surgery, but I have to tell you that the fractures are *not* the big concern. He's still bleeding but we can't intervene until we've stabilised his condition and this is the critical issue that we are monitoring. We've been giving him pain relief, and for the moment in addition to tube feeding him, we're just making him comfortable. I'm so sorry.'

Simon tried to take it all in, and then realised he had to ask the obvious question. He looked at the nurse and realised she was waiting for it.

'We're doing everything we can to make him comfortable right now, but if it was *my* dad, I'd be staying here for the time being. I can't really give you any more information at this time. If there *is* an improvement; and I have to caution you that we *don't* think that's likely, we should see it in the next few hours.'

'Thank you,' Simon whispered, and got up to return to the room his dad lay in.

Sally got up as he returned to the room. She'd always been there for them both, he realised; when his mum was ill, when she had passed away and now, ever reliable, ever loving, Sally was there for him again.

'Oh Sally,' he said, hugging the woman, 'Thank you for being here.'

She sniffed a little and indicated Ted, waiting outside, 'I've been here all night, so Ted has kindly said he'll take me home.

Do you want me to come back later on? I don't think you should be on your own, love.'

'Go home, get something to eat and some sleep. I'll stay here with him. I'll be fine. I'll call you if there's any change.'

She squeezed his hand and left.

***

Simon slung his jacket over the chair and sat again, stretching his legs out. A different nurse came in with a cup of tea for him and told him just to ring the bell if he needed anything. Then the two men were left alone.

Simon had left home shortly after his mum had died. He felt the need to get away and begin his own life, and quickly became a successful and popular builder. Then, of course, he met Jenn and, after a whirlwind romance and marriage they really didn't see Andrew much. Then with the inevitable marriage failure and pressure of business and then moving to France, Simon realised that now, in this hospital would probably be the most time he would now ever spend with his father, and it hurt dreadfully. All that *wasted* time, those wasted opportunities, and yet now; with all the time and nowhere to go, Simon couldn't tell his father all those things he wished he could.

With nothing to do, Simon inevitably started running through the events of the last couple of days. He would have to remain here in Bristol and see if his father improved, if they would then decide to operate on his hip, or if the worst was to happen, he'd have to wait and deal with his death. Back home…*Home*. What an evocative word that was. Where was home now? He thought France was his future, but now; if dad *did* recover he'd need to be here. He'd have to sort out a nursing home at the very least, and probably move back here to see to his recovery.

What about the whole poisoning thing back in St Honoré? He was still if not a suspect, then a witness, and possibly an intended victim. And what about the mill? He was responsible for paying the men and seeing to the renovation. They were almost half way through the project now - the project that would be of *so* much benefit to the village and to poor Émilie. He ran a hand over his eyes and tried to stop his brain churning everything over and over.

He looked over at his dad, lying so still; and remembered when his mother had died, when he was almost twenty. The cancer that she had concealed until the last two months had reduced her to skin and bone. Her once beautiful thick blonde hair had been cut short and her skin looked like old leaves. Simon used to sit with her reading to her when she wasn't sleeping and then finally, they'd taken her for her last week to a hospice. The house was at once empty and sad with too many things unsaid and hidden. Son and father mourned her and Andrew got on with life, throwing himself into work and never talking about her as it was too painful. That first Christmas was the toughest. Simon had disturbed him going through a box of her things. He'd been crying; really wailing, and Simon had rushed into their bedroom to find him holding her favourite scarf to his face, 'I'll never be able to smell her again,' he raised bloodshot puffy eyes to meet Simon's. 'She always used Chanel.'

They had clung to each other, crying. He remembered how hard it had been, then.

Simon sat and wiped away an angry tear.

'I can't even talk to you about her now, can I?' he gulped, standing up to stretch after the long drive.

He looked out of the window. The building was surrounded by houses and car parks, so different from his little village. Grey stone and concrete punctuated by small gardens and trees. Over to the West he could see where the apartment was where he'd previously lived with Jenn. It was now sold, after a brief status as the marital home. And to the right there was the little street where his parents had lived; where he'd been brought up.

He cast his eyes back to his dad; sleeping or just unconscious?

How could you *tell*? He sat again in the chair and held his father's hand. Suddenly, his stomach growled and he looked at his watch. God, he hadn't eaten for hours and it was now mid-afternoon. He gently returned his father's hand to the sheet and whispered, 'I'll be right back,' wondering why on earth he was whispering, as he went in search of the nurse.

She smiled and directed him to the canteen on the lower floor, promising to message him if anything changed. He sat in the busy canteen and ate a warm ham and cheese sandwich and a stale, but hot coffee. He took the opportunity to text a brief message to Philippe and to Émilie, and then returned back up to the ward.

The hours dragged by and still his father lay, unmoving. The beep, beep of the monitor was starting to play tricks with his brain and he paced the small room like a captive animal, weaving back and forth in front of the window.

Sally arrived at the end of visiting time with a bar of chocolate for Simon, and settled herself by Andrew's bed. She chatted away to the unresponsive man; telling him how the bus was late and the fact that the streets were packed in town.

Simon looked fondly at her. She'd always been there since mum had died, ready with a cuddle or a treat, and now she was making one-sided conversation with his remaining parent.

Suddenly the monitor failed, or was faulty. The beeping faltered. An alarm went off along at the nurse's station, and two nurses rushed in, one checking the monitor and lifting the emergency phone, the other trying to get Sally and Simon out of the small room.

'I just need to get some space to see to your dad', the big West Indian nurse said firmly, shoving him out. Two young doctors rushed past him, one pushing a trolley.

Simon's heart was racing as he tried to see what was happening. The alarm was turned off and the monitor quietened down. The doctor with the trolley came out again and without even a glance at Simon disappeared along the corridor.

Then the West Indian nurse came back out. She stood in front of Simon again, whilst the other nurse and doctor returned discreetly to their desk at the nurse's station.

'Mr Parker, come in and let me explain what's happening' she said quietly.

Andrew was still connected to the monitor, but his oxygen mask had been removed. Simon swallowed, and felt unable to breath; his heart felt as if it was in a vice.

'Mr Parker…Andrew has had a further relapse. We were worried this might happen, and I'm afraid *all* we can do is make him comfortable now. You can talk to him Simon. He isn't in pain, and I'm sure it will be a comfort to know you are here.'

Simon looked at her uncomprehending, 'Surely…'

She nodded her head slowly, 'I'm afraid so. Would you like me to call a priest?'

Simon caught a deep breath and a tear fell from his eye, which he brushed angrily away. He shook his head, unable to voice the jumbled thoughts going round his head. Sally was beside him and they instinctively found each other's hand, grasping tightly for comfort and reassurance. Simon sat on the edge of the bed and kissed his father's cheek.

'I love you dad. Always have. I have so much to tell you, if you'll wait. When you get better, I'll tell you all about France. You'd like it - no rain, nice food. Dad, I love you.' His voice faltered, and he gulped twice to hold back the anguish and heartbreak.

The nurse beckoned a crying Sally outside and Simon was left alone with his father. He sat there beside him, stroking his hair, murmuring 'I'm here. Everything's okay. I'm here. Don't go.' His tears started to fall freely, and he made no attempt to brush them away.

***

Andrew Parker slipped away silently as his son held his hand.

Chapter 14

The next two days were spent in a progression of trips to the registrar and the undertakers. Sally accompanied him and helped him choose flowers and hymns and rang round the dwindling numbers of relatives and a few friends to inform them of the funeral arrangements. Simon was still in shock at the suddenness of his father's death and found processing the experience surreal and callous. The registrar had *helpfully* given him a list of people he must contact including the Department of Works and Pensions, his GP and pension providers and Simon was working through them all in sequence, knowing that he'd have to return to France sometime soon. Grieving was apparently something you fitted in only when everything official had been taken care of.

Ted popped round to see him on the second evening, and arrived whilst Simon was gathering up the envelopes and paperwork that had filled the bureau. He was touched by Ted's visit, but dismayed at the conversation that followed. Ted had looked round the small living room at the boxes of paperwork and ephemera and sat on the sofa.

'Listen son, I'm you're dad's pal; we go way back, and I'm going to tell you how it is right now and you're not going to like it; but maybe you'll understand what I'm going to say in time.'

Simon poured them both the last of Andrew's bottle of malt. It was a 30 year old Aberlour that Simon had bought as a treat for him the previous Christmas. Ted swallowed it, took a deep breath and began an uncomfortable speech.

'You need to empty this house and sell it. Your life isn't here any more. You've a new life in France and Sally says you're happy there. There's nothing here for you now except ghosts of a past life. You can't live with ghosts, son; you're young and have your whole life ahead of you. Go home now that the funeral's organised, and when you come back you, me and Sally will go through your dad's things together. We'll take whatever's good to the charity shops and send the furniture to those people that help folk get started in council houses. Sell the house, son and go and live your life in France.'

Simon was dumbfounded and stared at Ted.

'I *know* it's harsh, but that's life. Life *is* harsh. I don't think he'd want you to keep this house. You need to take the good memories with you, with the photos and something to remember him and your mum by and go and *live*.'

He finished the whisky and stood up. 'I'm going now. I'll see you a day or so before the funeral. Go sort your watermill and I'll see you back here. And, Simon; I know it sounds awful; all this that I've said, but I'm right. You'll see that in time.'

Simon heard the door close but remained in the chair. His *dads* chair. His fingertips dug into the faded, slightly greasy arms and he looked round the tired and untidy room. Nothing had been changed or renewed since his mother had died. His dad had retreated into the past, living a little like Miss Haversham. Why hadn't he *seen* that before? He had probably; *definitely* been ill for years and Simon just hadn't noticed it. Hindsight was a wonderful thing, and he recalled his last visit when his dad had 'cooked' roast chicken from frozen. They'd laughed about it at the time; but the more Simon looked back, the more signs were there to tell, *if he had looked*. His parents were gone, and as he looked around the room, he realised Ted was right. There was nothing for him here in Bristol now. Tired and drained he fell asleep in the chair, feeling alone and unhappy.

***

The next morning he spoke to Sally after loading the car. He'd taken his grandfather's old wall clock from the living room, a box of photographs and a couple of boxes of bills and paperwork to go through when he was back in France. Sally had tearfully hugged him and then retreated back inside her house. With a last sad look at the house, he locked the door and drove off. He told Émilie much, much later that he'd managed to get around the corner of the street before he started crying and hadn't stopped until he'd reached the outskirts of Portsmouth.

***

Meanwhile, back in St Honoré, Philippe had taken charge of the building work at the mill. He'd taken the last two days off as holidays and was liaising with the *maire*, the architect and the heritage people to get a price for a brand-new artisan made wheel for the project. At night he sat with Émilie and the workmen, planning the following day's work and ensuring no-one was slacking whilst Simon was away. Even later at night Philippe kept a watchful eye on the buildings and an even closer eye on Jacques house. Everyone in the village knew of Simon's bereavement but also that, for the foreseeable future, Simon was on his way back to St Honoré, and the mill. What they discussed amongst themselves was whether he would now *stay* in France or return to the UK.

The village was also buzzing with the ghoulish gossip about the poisoning of the Englishman Barrie Curtis, who; following an emergency liver transplant was now tentatively expected to make a slow recovery. Never had the village so much to talk about. The television crew from the main news channel had arrived the day Simon left and finding very few people willing to be interviewed regarding the sensational events, stood in front of the *mairie* and the house of the poisoned man, expounding theories running from the reasonable to the ridiculous.

The police continued to interview many witnesses and worked behind the scenes making other more discreet enquiries.

Georges, the *maire* was busy trying to assist Sue Curtis as much as he could, whilst also highly involved in the mill project, visiting the heritage organisations and the tourist department in Périgueux when he could; coaxing and pleading for funding for the project.

***

Furiously disappointed and yet relieved not to have been questioned by the police, Jacques spent his time painting. Keeping out-of-sight he feverishly painted from morning till night, his nudes becoming more and more abstract and garish. Any real art lover would have seen that *something* was driving him and he painted like a man possessed. Jacques understood that his work was changing, improving. It was becoming more surreal, more fluid, and he thought, more like his hero Salvador Dali. He decided to increase his physical resemblance to the artist by painstakingly trimming and modelling his already ridiculously long moustaches, waxing them at the ends with a touch of soot to increase the colour. Bright and garish colour exploded on his canvases, and he convinced himself that these latest works were truly inspirational. The artist Dali was working *through* him; he was merely the conduit. In the summer heat he threw open the doors and windows to let in more light and from the street some tourists observed him painting furiously. A few even approached to watch and finally, he sold one of the canvases to a very enthusiastic American, who didn't even baulk at his off-the-cuff price of 300 euros. Of course, that just turned his head completely, and he spent the entire, outrageous amount on replacement paint and canvases.

***

The *maire* was annoyed that so far the police had not interviewed whom he considered the prime suspect. His calls to see what progress was being made in the case were politely acknowledged, but he was informed that the case was proceeding and they had no information to give him at this time.

In fact the police were busy. They had many witness statements placing Jacques Bordes at the scene; in fact at the very table where the victim had been sitting, so the police *could* establish opportunity. But they needed much more. The evidence of the poisonous fungi was long-gone; the police only had the toxicology report to attest to the poisoning; the motive was at this point flimsy – the actual victim now appeared not to have been the originally *intended* victim; and to put the case to court, the police needed concrete evidence. And this was their main problem - no-one had actually witnessed the contamination of the pizza. It was becoming clear that the poisoning of Mr Curtis was a mistake, and that Simon Parker was the intended victim all along. And so they waited; refusing to interview their prime suspect; their *only* suspect for the time being, and hoped that more information; more *evidence* would be forthcoming. The detective in charge of the case was anxious; this approach was fraught with danger. By allowing the main suspect to remain at large, there was a risk that he would think he'd slipped through the net; that he would be tempted to make another, possibly *successful* attempt on the Englishman's life.

He picked up his phone and arranged for a small detail of plain clothes men to be stationed around the village. Posing as tourists they would blend in at this time of year and keep an eye on things. The last attempt had been a close thing; he didn't want to risk a successful pre-meditated murder in the height of the tourist season.

***

Oblivious to all that was going on regarding the investigation, Simon Parker drove down through the French countryside towards the small village he had called home. He stopped at Les Eyzies to buy a filled baguette and stretch his legs and then continued on, finally arriving in the late evening at the old mill. He'd telephoned Philippe ahead and was grateful to find a new outside light outside the cottage welcoming him and his fridge filled with some bottled water, beer, a bottle of rosé wine and some basic groceries. The vase beside his bed was filled with roses and his bathroom was now fully tiled and functional. He took a long shower which helped wash away the grime and sweat of the journey and eased his tense shoulders, before falling exhausted into bed.

****

Philippe watched from the road. His friend had returned and tomorrow was soon enough to talk. Tonight he would sleep, and hopefully sleep would kindly give him some solace. The last week had been more than enough to test any man, and Philippe wondered if the Englishman's resolve had weakened. Would he stay? Would he, now free of any inducement to return to his old home fully embrace making St Honoré his new home? They had much to discuss. Tomorrow. He sighed and turned away from the *moulin* and walked home. He was tired. Tired of pushing the workman to work unsupervised; tired of Georges the *maire's* wavering loyalty in the face of village gossip, and tired of waiting for Jacques Bordes to make a mistake. The police, an unpopular but necessary evil in society were *too* slow; the longer they took, the more chance; now that Simon had returned, that he would again become the focus of the vendetta that could *next time*, kill him. Philippe was convinced that Jacques would indeed try again. With two previous attempts, he was certain of this; and unknown to him, this was *exactly* what the police detective in charge of the case also believed.

****

The sun rose hot and fierce, and Simon awoke to the sound of a bell being rung. He opened his eyes, and had to adjust for a moment. He was in his own bed. But the bell he heard was *not* one of the church bells. He got up and pulled on a pair of shorts and walked stiffly downstairs. Émilie was standing at the door with a basket of bread, almond croissants and fresh milk. With the sun behind her highlighting the copper tints in her dark hair and her golden tan, she looked the embodiment of health and goodness; and she was smiling at him. She placed the basket on the kitchen table and walked into his waiting arms, dispelling all the sadness and weariness and filling him with love and belonging. They stood silently for a few moments, hugging fiercely before she pulled away. 'Later,' she said, and blew him a kiss, before leaving.

He followed her to the door, watching her walk quickly back to the *boulangerie*. It was then he noticed the small brass bell hanging from a chain at the side of the door beside the new light. He smiled to himself and returned to make some coffee and enjoy a proper breakfast.

A few minutes later, Philippe arrived and the two men embraced for a long moment.

'I am so sorry,' he said simply and accepted a proffered coffee.

Simon smiled sadly and unable to find any words, did what any good Frenchman would do and shrugged. Between such friends words are not needed and they sat, quietly drinking coffee until the workmen started to arrive.

After the welcomes and condolences, Simon decided they needed to have a talk, and he proposed coffee at the *Salamandre* in five minutes before they resumed work on the mill. They left him to dress and when he walked over to meet with them, was pleased to see the *maire* also in attendance.

He formally expressed his thanks to everyone for continuing the work on the cottage and mill and informed them that they would be pressing on with the renovations, including dredging the pit that the wheel would eventually sit in. They were relieved to know that nothing had changed, and that apart from returning to the UK for a few days to attend the funeral, Simon Parker was just as committed to finishing the work on the mill. The men returned to their work, and Philippe and Georges updated Simon with the progress of the applications for heritage funding, the plans for a new mill wheel and the installation of the now necessary extra septic tank behind the mill building.

'The tank is coming next week, and I have arranged the excavator to come and install then, but the old agricultural machinery that is sitting round the back will need to be moved out of the way for the operator. Perhaps when he is here we can get him to dredge the mill wheel pit, but the mill wheel itself will be a few months. The expert from the Federation of Mills has been for a visit. He's happy with most of the machinery, but a new wheel takes a long time to make, but the good news is that they've agreed to fund it.'

Philippe was pleased to impart some good news, but Georges, eager not to be outdone then piped up, '*And* the Department will fund the laying of a new *chemin* in Asphalt and a parking area. *Don't* ask me how I managed this…' he grinned, tapping his nose.

'You *have* been busy.' Simon finally answered, relieved that some funding was coming and that the men had judiciously taken care of some of the things that needed to be moved on. 'Thank you. That's a lot off my mind.' He took a deep breath, 'Now, we need to talk about the *other thing*. Has anyone heard about Barrie?'

Georges explained that Barrie was on the slow route to recovery with a new liver and that the surgeons were cautious about his recovery and the future. Sue was coping, and the commune was looking after them both. They expected Barrie to be released from hospital towards the end of the month.

The police investigation was ongoing, Philippe told him. The three of them sat silently and it hung between them; an unspoken almost tangible barrier. No-one wanted to talk about it and they each retreated for a few moments into themselves whilst they drank coffee. Finally, it was Simon who broke the uneasy silence, 'I'm selling my father's home and this will be my home. I'm not going to be chased away, and think I can make a new life here. *If* I'm allowed.'

Georges shook his head sadly, 'I've never experienced *anything* like this, and I'm sure this is the end of all the unpleasantness. At least you seem to be exonerated by the police, thank God. So – their investigation continues and we must wait. Jacques is still free, although he seems to be behaving; at least he is keeping out of everyone's way and is painting like a madman...' he stopped, wishing he'd not used that word, but then carried on, 'and we are being *very* vigilant. I can only hope you will put the actions of one individual behind you, and if not forgive, then forget.'

Simon thought that highly unlikely, but said nothing. George stood to go, 'I must return to the *mairie*; so much to do...' He shook Simon's hand and then Philippe's, and left the veranda of the almost silent bar.

Philippe broke the silence, 'My friend, I must return to my work tomorrow, but be assured that I am always here for you, and you must come to me if you need anything. I think Georges only sees what he wants to see regarding the nature of people, but you must remain watchful. I think the police are waiting, and so must we. I fear this problem with Jacques will not vanish. I am convinced now that he *is* a madman.'

Simon was glad he wasn't the only one thinking this. Now that he'd returned, he'd need to be on his guard, day and night. They walked back to the top of the *chemin* and Simon bid his friend farewell, 'I need to get some work done, and tonight, I'll see Émilie. It's good to be back.'

The men worked till after six and one by one said their goodbyes; some with expressions of condolence and some just welcoming him back. At the end of the working day Simon locked the tools away and tidied up. As he was finishing,

Émilie appeared in a pretty shell-pink dress, announcing that dinner would be on the table in twenty minutes and that he just had time for shower. He looked down at himself and realised he was filthy. He nodded and she turned quickly and left. He hoped nothing was amiss, and headed for the bathroom. In less than twenty minutes he was clean, dressed and just before he left the cottage, noted the small table lamp in the living room had been plugged into a timer. Someone; either Philippe or Émilie had made sure that it appeared that the cottage was not empty whilst he was away. This small courtesy pleased him, and feeling emotional and tired, he began to walk to the *boulangerie* and his waiting girl.

Chapter 15

The table in the kitchen was set for two with pretty floral plates, glasses and a large basket of bread. Pots on the cooker top hissed and bubbled and a delicious mélange of aromas filled the air. Émilie had her long curly hair tied back in a ponytail and was standing at the stove with her back to him wearing short shorts, and revealing her long tanned legs. She heard him in the doorway and turned, ignored his hungry eyes travelling up and down her form, (although she was secretly delighted) and pushed a glass of cold white wine into his hand and ordered him to sit.

'Eat first,' she commanded with a saucy smile, as she began to fill his plate with pink slivers of lamb and small salad potatoes cooked with garlic and mushrooms, adding a large ladleful of cauliflower cheese. He didn't need to be told twice and the first bite of his favourite (how did she know?) cauliflower cheese was a delight to his senses. Just perfectly cooked with an intriguing mix of melted strong cheese and slightly crunchy topping. He closed his eyes in ecstasy.

'It's the topping,' she giggled as she took in his delighted smile. 'Tiny breadcrumbs and parmesan cheese at the last minute under the grill.'

He nodded his approval and tried the small bite-sized potatoes just competing gently with fat cooked whole cloves of garlic, and a sprinkling of finely chopped spring onions. He was about to pop one large juicy mushroom into his mouth when the whole poisoning episode suddenly came flooding back and he stopped and looked at her and then the mushroom on his fork; eyebrows raised.

'Oh *now* you think I am going to poison you?' she laughed archly, 'Before I take you to my bed and show you how much I have missed you, *chéri*? Don't be silly! Now EAT!'

He never spoke again until he had finished wiping the plate clean with a chunk of the delicious bread and downed the last of the white wine.

'That has to be one of the best meals I've ever had', he said, pushing the plate away. 'The cauliflower cheese was *amazing*; how did you know it was my favourite?'

She shrugged a shoulder and smiled, 'You are English and the English love their Sunday roast; I cannot make those silly pudding things, but I can make nice *gratin*, I think.'

She got up and cleared the plates and brought some warm *tarte tatin;* with a thin short-crust pastry base, and the top covered with caramelised apple slices and a sticky glaze, finished with a spoonful of thick cream. She sat to join him again, and the two ate silently, their eyes meeting over the table, remembering what it was like to be together and alone, and feeling the frisson of excitement and longing between them.

'Café?' she just managed to ask with a slightly wicked smile, and walked to the counter as if to begin the ritual of coffee making, but Simon came up behind her, wrapping his arms around her, and inhaling her scent as if he'd been away from her for a lifetime. He buried his face in her hair, feeling her press her body against him.

'Émilie. Dear sweet Émilie, God I've missed you so much.' He began to kiss her neck and she took his hand and led him upstairs to the bedroom. This time, she undressed in front of him, slowly and simply, letting her clothes fall to the floor. Then, she reached for him and began slowly to unbutton his shirt. Oblivious to the outside world, the lovers slowly began to rediscover each other, each trying to please the other, with occasional gasps and squeals of delight.

Downstairs, Eloise curled up in her basket and sighed. She

wondered if she might actually get a walk tonight; but content with the leftover dinner scraps, she settled down to sleep.

When it was dark, much, *much* later and Émilie had returned from allowing the dog to have a short walk around her small garden, Simon lay watching her with his head resting on his arm. 'I'm *not* going home,' he announced, 'I'm staying here with you all night.'

Laying down besides him, she let her long hair spill out over his chest, and looked up at his face,

'I should think not', she smiled, 'After all, I need to ensure that if we are to continue this romance, I need to know exactly what I can expect from you in bed. So tonight, I will enjoy you all night, until I have to begin work.'

'Well, I hope I don't disappoint,' he laughed, 'but I have to tell you that I'm out of practice and probably wont come up to scratch compared to what you may expect from a Frenchman.'

'I have all night to teach you everything I know, and you can teach me tomorrow night,' she purred, sliding her hands up and down his body gently, 'Practise makes perfect.'

Simon offered up a silent fervent prayer and then excitedly turned his full attention to his teacher.

***

It was far too soon when she crept quietly from the bed and went for a shower. Dawn was only just lightening the sky outside the window. She returned damp and naked and began to tease him with tiny kisses to her lips and neck. He groaned and begged her to come back, but she was resolute.

'You are insatiable, but I must go and begin the bread. Lie here a while and I'll bring you some coffee and then you also need to get on with your day. Tonight, I will come to you. *You* will cook for me and then ...' she wiggled her eyebrows and raised her arms to brush and tie up her hair.

Simon marvelled at her. She really was the most beautiful, sexy, maddening woman he'd ever had the luck to know. She slipped her clothes on quickly and then, from the door, she blew him a kiss and tiptoed down the stairs. He closed his eyes for a few seconds to remember and relish their lovemaking, and then, it seemed like just a few minutes later, she was shaking his shoulder and presenting him with coffee and *pain au chocolat.*

'Seven, and you'd better move, or we will be the talk of the village, yet again!' she laughed, and ran back downstairs.

He jumped out of bed and headed for the shower.

When Josiane Cholet arrived at the *boulangerie* a few minutes later for her bread, she was convinced she could hear singing…*from upstairs*? Her eyes followed the sound and clever Émilie turned the radio in the *boulangerie* up a little louder.

'It's going to be another beautiful day, *n'est pas*?' she smiled broadly.

The old lady behind her in the queue nudged Josiane, 'I wish I could have a little of what *she* has to make her so happy at this time in the morning.'

'I *bet* you do,' murmured Josiane with a giggle; correctly guessing at what had put the glow into Émilie Fournier's complexion before briskly taking her bread and her gossip home to her husband.

***

Working with a spring in his step, Simon didn't feel tired until lunch time, and then exhaustion hit him. He realised with a start that he hadn't thought about his poor dad since dinner last evening and felt guilty and sad. He missed him of course, but the father-child relationship had fizzled out a few years previously and Simon recalled that when they had been together, they really didn't talk about much and had nothing in common. He supposed that's what happened when you grew up and made your own way in life, and vowed to remember the good times and to look out and get the reels of cine film uploaded into a form he could watch and enjoy.

150

Then he remembered with a start that he'd have to shop to cook a dinner for Émilie; and he didn't have a clue what to cook! Everyone in France seemed to be able to produce wonderful meals from simple ingredients and it must be absorbed in the home as they grew up, but for Simon; a builder who could exist on ready meals or sandwiches, he realised he was on a steep learning curve and would need to spend the rest of the afternoon preparing.

***

He changed and jumped into his car and headed to the large supermarket in Sarlat, where he had an interesting conversation with the butcher behind the counter, who was trying to recommend some sort of dish with veal. Simon hesitated and decided veal wasn't going to cut it so he then headed to the fish counter; and intending to buy some oysters, fell into conversation with the fishmonger.

'You want something light - perhaps to start a small plate of *fruit de mer*. You won't need to cook anything – it's ready to go, just arrange on a large plate with some ice, and a basket of bread, and a cold bottle of white wine. Then honey and garlic salmon.'

She helpfully wrote the recipe down and told Simon where to find the additional ingredients he needed.

'And to conclude, either a small cheeseboard or something with chocolate. You can't go wrong with either. And a half bottle of *Monbazillac* sweet white wine with the dessert. So romantic! And I thought the English didn't understand romance!' she laughed and handed over the bags of food and with a wave, wished him '*Bon chance*.'

***

The rest of the afternoon was spent setting the scene. On the way home, he collected a bouquet of flowers from the florist in St Cyprien and arranged them in a vase in the living room. The windows were flung open to air the room, and he vacuumed, made the bed up and cleaned the bathroom. The seafood was arranged on a sharing plate, and placed in the fridge, and he began, with some trepidation to cook the salmon.

Every few minutes the workmen would interrupt to ask something about the mill renovation, and then got sidetracked by his cooking and remained a few minutes to give him their advice.

'Have you *thoroughly* boned that salmon?' Jojo commented looking critically at the fish. Simon chased him.

'That cheeseboard will not be big enough,' Claude said fifteen minutes later, when coming to confirm the sizes of the sack-hatch doors.

'It's for *two* people!' Simon exclaimed, looking at the large chunks of four different cheeses.

'Ah, but when you have eaten, and then later…when you are hungry after making love, you may feel in need of nourishment again…' Claude commented, wiggling his eyebrows.

'Get OUT!' Simon chased him with a dishcloth.

***

The men disappeared at six, wishing him luck and success, and Simon; after checking and double-checking that he had done everything, and forgotten nothing, decided to take the opportunity to have a shower.

He was enjoying the feel of warm water and soap cascading down his body when he delightedly realised he wasn't alone, and the girl; this beautiful seductress had stepped naked into the shower beside him. All thoughts of dinner flew from his mind and they giggled as they soaped each other slowly.

'You are a witch, woman,' he finally said and stepped from the shower to grab thick rough towels to dry them both off. Then, with his blood on fire, he threw the towels to the floor and carried her laughing to his bed and threw her down, ignoring her squeals that the sheets would get wet. 'Stuff the sheets', he

152

growled and began to feast on her body as she arched to meet him.

Just as well the dinner would wait, she murmured some time later.

***

Meanwhile, Josiane Cholet was serving up ratatouille to her husband, who had returned home dusty and tired from his days work. She twittered around him as she poured his *rosé* wine, gossiping that Émilie was not at the *boulangerie* this evening, but probably at the mill with Simon; and that Georges had called in earlier to check that the old agricultural equipment would be moved from the rear of the mill where the new *fosse* was to be installed, but Philippe just ate quietly. He loved his wife dearly, but a man just wanted to eat his dinner in peace, he remarked once, signalling for more bread.

Josiane was impatient to gossip and despite her husbands obvious fatigue and hunger, could not resist a further attempt at starting a conversation about the new romance.

She sat down opposite him with a tiny flounce, banging the basket of bread in front of him.

'*Well?*'

'Well, what?'

'Aren't you going to go see him and check that the things are moved?'

'Not tonight. He's entertaining, I believe.'

She stared at him, comprehension and excitement making her eyes shine.

'Ooooh!'

'Yes; ooooh. Now shut up woman, and pour more wine.'

***

In the morning, Philippe walked round to the mill. Simon was up, dressed and in the kitchen, washing up the pots and pans from the night before. The door was open, but Philippe coughed

153

and tapped the doorframe politely to draw his attention.

Simon turned and smiled, beckoning him in.

The men sat at the table and discussed moving the agricultural equipment. The grass had grown around it all and Simon would need to strim much of it down before they could see what exactly was there and if it could be moved by hand. If not, Philippe would come round after work with his tractor and they'd pull it out. There needed to be clear space for the excavator to both dig the pit and to pile the excavated soil.

'When do you return to England?' Philippe asked finally.

'Next Tuesday. The funeral is on Thursday and I'll have to get the house valued and put on the market. I'm going to take the car to bring some things back. I've got a few days to empty the place, but my father's friends have offered to help. It'll be hard, getting rid of so many memories, and so much stuff.'

He sat quietly. It would probably appear that he was dealing with his father's sudden death very brusquely, but he didn't think it had really registered with him yet. When everything had calmed down he would really miss his father, and be able to mourn him properly, but it all seemed like a completely different world now; England, Bristol and his father. Simon had settled in this quaint little village and was happier here, especially now that he and Émilie were strengthening the ties between them.

'And you have heard nothing from the police since you returned?' Philippe asked bluntly, bursting Simon's happy bubble.

'No.'

'I think you still need to be on your guard, my friend.'

Simon knew exactly who he was referring to, and shook his head. 'I disagree. He's had his chance and failed again. That'll be the end of it. Everyone thinks it was him; he'd be a fool to try anything now.'

'I must go; I have a long day, but will call round this evening, if you will be here?'

Simon caught the smile in his voice and smiled back. 'Yes, I'll be here. Alone. If I was a younger man, I'd be at Émilie's, but she's wearing me out!' he laughed.

'It is good to see you both happy, but just …well, take your time. You have the rest of your lives together, I think. And keep watch.'

And with that, Philippe drained the last of the coffee and was gone.

***

The workmen arrived and a couple helped Simon with the strimming and they pulled out an old wooden cart, mostly rotten, but not completely ruined. With some repairs, it would make a nice feature in the garden. A large iron hay tedder was also released from the vegetation and pulled to the front of the barn, adjoining the mill. Spines facing the sky, it rested easily on the old fashioned and uncomfortable looking iron seat. Then a couple of old wooden wine barrels, which Simon thought might be re-purposed as water-butts if they were watertight. Claude filled them with water to see if the staves would swell and seal any leaks. After this they began working on the upper floor of the mill, following the complicated plans provided by the mill federation. There were many belts and pulleys to be installed when they were nearer completion, but the floor hatches had to be fitted to prevent any accidents.

When the men left Simon heated up a pizza in the new range in the kitchen and threw a salad together. With some rosé wine, he settled himself outside to eat and to watch the geese on the other side of the *étang*. It was odd that he was actually now using many French words instead of the English translation, and he wondered if it was normal. After all, it was now the start of July and he had been living here a good few months with no other English people to converse with. He listened and tried to remember everything and could now hold a reasonable conversation with the French, but school-book French and

155

everyday French were very different things, he smiled. He decided to walk over to the *Salamandre* after his pizza and pass the early evening with Henri and Marie before having an early night.

They talked about everything and yet nothing important; of the increasing numbers of visitors, the weather, and inevitably the coming school holidays. After a few glasses of wine, he waved goodbye and walked slowly back in the twilight to the cottage with its welcoming light.

A barn owl flew silently past him; a soft white shadow in the dusk, heading for the old barn next to the mill. Simon stood and watched it land in the open hoist window and retreat inside. Perhaps he could construct some kind of box for it, as they would be good at keeping the mice and any rats down. He stretched and pushed the cottage door open. It was good to be home. On the table in the living room was a framed photo of his mum and dad. Taken when they were both newly married, they were smiling and happy, and Simon felt pleased that, in some form, they were joining him here in France in his lovely watermill. He said goodnight to them sadly and wearily climbed the stairs to bed, pulling the pillow that now smelt of jasmine and honeysuckle to his cheek before he fell deeply asleep.

Chapter 16

The next few days were busy with work. Simon and his workmen marked out the area behind the mill where the new *fosse septique* would be installed, and also where the spoil would be deposited. The excavator operator visited to survey the access and the excavation job itself and agreed to also dredge out the mill pit at the same time for a small extra cash fee. Georges brought a couple of members of the committee from The Mills Federation, who took many photographs of the progress of the project and confirmed that funding had been found for the new mill wheel. They were in no hurry to leave, and hung around admiring the building so much so that Simon had to make his excuses and carry tools upstairs through the granary floor of the mill through to the connecting upper floor of the barn.

He found the barn owl roosting at the dark far end, and decided that work on the barn would have to wait until they had figured out what was essential so as not to disturb the creature. In the past this building would have been multi-purpose. Grain and flour stored upstairs in the *bin* or granary floor, which was open to the upper floor of the mill workings in the main mill building; and either horses or agricultural equipment in the ground floor of the barn. There was no evidence of woodworm which surprised him, until one of the mill experts explained that sweet chestnut timber was used in many important buildings because insects did not like it. In fact, he remarked that Simon should endeavour to also use the same as in the long run it would not need any treatment, be in keeping with a sympathetic restoration and cheaper overall.

Simon was more concerned at the state of the stonework around the opening in the upper barn level, where the sacks would be hoisted in and out. The stones appeared loose; probably having been frequently bashed against by the weight of sacks of grain and other things, and would need to be removed and re-bedded with lime cement and then re-pointed. But that would have to wait. He needed to concentrate on the present issues of organising the installation of the *fosse*. The plumbers were busy routing foul water pipes to the rear of the building and complaining that their drill bits simply weren't long enough to penetrate through the wall, which was more than a metre thick. Clever Jojo overheard this and rooted around in the rubble heap near the *chemin*, before returning with a length of steel rod. He dragged Simon's welding equipment from the shed and an hour later presented the plumbers with two extended bits; explaining that they needed to drill for a short time and keep the hole wet to cool the drill bits.

***

Émilie meanwhile was trying to juggle baking and serving with enduring the flashy *immobilier* showing round a couple who were interested in buying the *boulangerie* building and turning it into an *épicerie*, or grocery store. They seemed sympathetic to her situation; which she explained in front of the *immobilier*, who was quietly furious in case he lost a sale; but the couple explained that as the village didn't have a grocery shop they would not be any competition to her. Furthermore, they were looking at an entry date of the end of October. That gave her almost a full four months. She would of course have to wait to see if the sale did in fact materialise, and this on one hand would mean that the shared asset with her soon-to-be ex-husband would be dealt with, whilst on the other, it would force her to look at moving the business and her home. The mill was years away from full flour production, but she could run the *boulangerie* from there. She'd need to speak to Simon later.

***

Lunchtime came and went and the men dealt with a delivery of timber for the upper mill floor, and they hoisted the wood up and through the open double shuttered window opening above the main mill door This was a long process as they still had to replace the actual hoist mechanism, which over time, overuse and weather was now creaking and shuddering with any substantial weight. They couldn't use the other hoist on the barn, as this was blocked outside with the agricultural equipment that had been moved there to allow the excavator to install the *fosse*.

***

The heat was building through the day and tempers were getting a little frayed. As it was Friday, and the following Monday was the French equivalent to Whitsun holiday, Simon decided to send them home early, and by three o'clock he was alone at the mill, sitting in the shade with his laptop, trying to balance the books and responding to messages of condolence or regrets that they were unable to attend his dad's funeral.

Jojo called round with his wife and children in the car, mentioning to Simon that the holiday weekend would be ideal to start the fencing of the meadow for the impending movement of his sheep to enjoy the lush grass, which Simon had completely forgotten about. A few friends would help him and he thought that they would be finished and the sheep in residence by the time Simon returned from England.

Simon was cheered by this and looked at planning the short, sad but necessary trip back to the UK. He phoned Sally and a couple of his dad's old friends and arranged to meet everyone at the house on Wednesday to begin sorting through the decades of belongings. He was dreading it, he realised and felt morose.

159

Still, it had to be done, and as he planned on having as short a trip as was necessary, he then telephoned and arranged three estate agents to do valuations on the Friday; the day after the funeral, feeling it was better to at least get on with the inevitable.

***

Émilie arrived around five, and insisted on dragging him away from the *moulin* and his thoughts and they drove to a small bend at the nearby river Vezere where they stripped off and swam in the clear, clean waters before drying themselves on a shady bank. It was just the therapy he needed, and they lay in the meadow surrounded by butterflies and dragonflies and watched the kites wheel above them in the sky.

She told him of the visit to the *boulangerie* by the prospective new owners, and he immediately suggested that when she knew something concrete, just to start moving her belongings into the cottage. They lay entwined in the grass, happy to be together and he began to relax. They decided to eat at the *Salamandre* that evening, and the next day would visit the large wood-yard to choose the wood that would be milled ready to make the counter tops and door fronts for the units in the new shop in the ground floor of the mill. Émilie had already chosen the modern kitchen units for the storage at the rear of the commercial kitchen and she would deal with the orders for this whilst he was in England.

***

The next few days came and went at blinding speed. The couple chose some oak and took a sample home to check it against the existing wood in the large ground floor space that was to become the mill, and then spent some time in the garden, with Émilie supervising him as they worked together. Jojo and his friends arrived and the air was filled with the sounds of the tractor and post basher thumping-in sweet chestnut fence posts all round the meadow. The geese honked and hissed loudly and Jacques made his first appearance for many weeks, gesticulating wildly and loudly at the noise and disturbance. Jojo later told Simon that the man looked awful; even dirtier and drunker than normal, with a wild look in his eyes.

On Monday night, after he'd hung his suit in the back of the pick-up and thrown in a small bag, Émilie covered his face with little kisses and cried a little as he began the long drive back to Bristol. He'd presented her theatrically with the keys to the property and told her that she was now in charge. The sudden silence that filled the dark, warm night was oppressive and she walked back into the cottage with a shiver, and sat feeling a little lonely for a few minutes on the sofa with Eloise, who had made the cottage her second home. But Eloise; sensing the girl's need for companionship and love, cuddled into her side on the sofa, and when Émilie finally mounted the stairs to go to bed, Eloise followed her up and onto the previously forbidden bed, where she was cuddled all night.

***

The funeral was a blustery event with that ever-permeating drizzle that you only seem to find in Britain. Almost imperceptible it soaked through clothing and made everyone miserable. Despite the threatening dark clouds and gusts of wind, his dad had a good turnout and the funeral tea afterwards in an old but elegant Bristol hotel was well attended by friends, and old work colleagues. A couple of Simon's cousins had dutifully come to pay their respects, but Simon hadn't seen them for many years and discovered they had little in common. Everyone drifted off by five o'clock and Simon drove Sally back to her house. He refused her kindly offer of dinner and a bed, having set his mind on staying in his dad's house that night and they'd start the difficult business of sorting Andrew's belonging's the next morning.

The next two days were countless trips to charity shops and the council rubbish tip. Ted had told him to be ruthless; that he'd have to sort realistically what needed kept and what was just basically rubbish. Everything in the kitchen cupboards was boxed and taken to the charity shop, all the unused medicine returned to the pharmacy for disposal and Sally cleaned out the fridge and cooker which were to be sold. They unearthed a huge pile of old women's magazines in the under the stairs cupboard from the 1960's, which he realised must have been his mothers; and he filled two bin bags with them. Old worn towels, bedding and such-like packed into the car and taken away, personal items agonised over and then again removed. It was mind-blowingly tedious and depressing. On his last trip to the tip on the second day he told Sally and Ted to take anything they wanted from what was left. He'd had enough for the time being. Estate agents came, measured, photographed and left; he'd have their valuations in a day or so. A trip to the family lawyer explained his father's will and the probate process, and he agreed to deal with the sale of the house.

***

This is what life comes down to, Simon thought sadly. Those who remain after a death are left to sift through belongings and memories that had taken years to make, and they are sorted almost callously and instantaneously in order to move on. Sally was cross with him as he voiced this, but she didn't put up a counter argument.

Most of the house was finally emptied by the third day, leaving his dads chair and Simon's bed in his old room upstairs. His car was stuffed full of boxes of paperwork and photographs and old cine film he discovered by chance in a box in the loft.

All cut and dried. A life neatly and efficiently processed, he reflected grimly. He slept that final night in his old bed, before handing the house key over to Sally the next morning, who'd agreed to watch over it, and deal with any mail until Simon returned. He was vague about this, and she understood why, so didn't press him, and he finally drove away, shaking the drizzle and depression from himself with every mile he drove towards home.

***

The car was heavy and slow, and after disembarking from the ferry he slowly pulled out of the port and headed south. It was evening now and he decided to drive all night again. He told himself because it was cooler and the traffic much reduced, but deep down he really just wanted to be at home again. The skies remained clear and the crescent moon kept him company as he negotiated bends and turns and junctions. The headlights attracted some bats as he drove, and on one occasion they picked out the shadowy forms of a couple of roe deer grazing at the side of a quiet road.

Eventually the sky lightened, and his spirits rose with the sun which filled the sky with a rosy glow. He glanced at his watch and thought that seven am was not too early for breakfast, and began to look for a reasonably sized village to eat. Tractors forced him to reduce his speed as they began their working day and then he spied a village, and stopped at a small bakery to eat, stretch his legs and change into a tee shirt and shorts. The further south he drove, the better he felt, and as he headed down the D706 Vezere Valley road, he had shaken off the depression of the last few days and welcomed the sounds of France Bleu radio, playing the cringworthy but upbeat Eurotrash tunes that told him he was nearly home.

***

As he entered St Honoré, he was waved at by the children in the school playground and he slowed down and honked his horn to their shrieks of delight. Georges was standing beside one of the commune's little work vans talking to the driver and responded with a vigorous wave, calling to him, '*Le Salamandre ce soir*?'

Simon gave him the thumbs up and drove down the small *chemin* to the mill. *Le Vieux Moulin,* now boasted a new laser-

163

cut sign besides his post box. Small lavender bushes had been planted on either side of the *chemin*, and beautiful Émilie was waiting for him at the door, with Eloise on a long chain tied outside. He jumped from the cab and embraced her warmly.

'Has that dog been naughty again?' he asked when he'd finally stopped kissing her.

'*Au contraire*, she has been my watchdog here,' she said with a tight smile and ordered him inside to rest.

He waited for her to snuggle next to him and then listened as she explained that two nights ago Eloise had run to the door barking and growling. She had put on the outside lights and gone outside, but there was nothing, and nobody to be seen.

Simon sighed, 'Maybe a cat, or that owl, or the geese, or the frogs…We can't just assume that that mad nutter was prowling around.'

Her expression showed that she didn't believe any of it and merely said, 'She may be a small dog, but she has a big bite. Next time I will let her out, *then* we shall see!'

He laughed and hugged her again, before standing up,

'I'm sorry love, I must be stinking. I'll go and have a shower and then we can talk properly.'

'I will make some coffee and we can sit in the shade outside, not that there is much room out there with all this farming machinery. I'll be glad when it is all round the back again.'

He returned a few minutes later with damp hair and clean clothes and sat with her outside. She'd evidently made some *macarons,* which he ate greedily till when he reached for the third one she slapped his hand. 'You'll get fat. I will be living with a fat man. My mother will despair! A fat Englishman!' she laughed and rolled her eyes.

'I work too hard to get fat!' he answered and downed the last of the coffee.

'So, be a good girl and tell me what you've been up to and what everyone else has been up to. Remember, when I first met you, you told me you "*know everything and everybody*". So, what's been happening here whilst I've been away?'

***

Once Simon had told her briefly about the funeral and clearing the house they changed the subject to a happier one, and spent the next hour chatting and laughing, each updating the other, with Simon gradually yawning and feeling drowsy. 'I'll leave you to have a little sleep and come back later and make dinner,' she volunteered.

He took the opportunity to bring up the subject of their relationship, and to finally tell her in detail how he felt.

'I don't want you ever to leave me Émilie. I need to know that we are going to make a real go of this – of the joint mill and bakery thing, but more importantly, I want us to live together. I think we could make each other happy. I know its fast, but I've never felt more sure in my life. I love you; *really* love you and care about you. I want to spend the rest of my life here *with you*. It's as simple as that. Please just stay. Move in here and stay.'

The girl stood stock still, staring at him, measuring him. The English – so different from the French; so eager, so quick to commit. She didn't want to give him an answer just yet, so she played for time; 'Will you agree to meet my mother? She is coming to visit next week? I *might* consider permanently moving in if she approves of you?' she smiled impishly.

'Of course! Alright, I'll let you come round to the idea in your own time, whilst you savagely use me nightly for sex, but one day Émilie Fournier, you *will* fall head over heels in love with me too!'

She turned on one delectable foot and opened the door, 'I will see you in *Le Salamandre* for dinner at seven, set your alarm. And we will not be alone. Half the village want to welcome you back.'

She started to leave and then from the safety of the doorway turned her smiling face back to him, 'Savagely use you for sex

165

nightly?' She rolled her eyes, grinned and blew him a long kiss and then was gone.

Chapter 17

He slept for a couple of hours and woke refreshed, but hungry. He unloaded some of the stuff from his car and put it in the spare bedroom. In the coming months he would go through the photographs and things, but not today. He had some time to wander around before meeting his friends at the bar and slipping on his sandals decided to check the place over. He admired the small lavender plants, already flowering and filling the air with scent, and noted that the grass to the side of the cottage was neatly cut and that some new clay pots had arrived and were spilling over with red geraniums. As he walked past the barn that adjoined the mill he had to detour around the hay tedder and old cart, but was delighted to see that water level in the *étang* had dropped and realised that Philippe must have raised the *vannes* supplying the mill race and diverted the water down the overflow leat, so that the pit; that would in future house the new wheel was empty, although muddy. This was one of the jobs they would tackle this week; removing years of sludge and debris to see the exact depth of the pit for the measurement of the new wheel and to ascertain if repairs were required to the pit walls.

***

Next to the *étang* the meadow had been fenced with chestnut stakes, with a gate at the top of the *chemin*. Some pretty Causses sheep were quietly grazing within. He liked the look of them with their curious friendly faces, big ears and large black eye patches. They'd been shorn recently and looked clean and comfortable in their new home as they allowed their already large lambs to suckle occasionally, whilst they converted the lush meadow grass into protein. The loud and aggressive geese were still on guard duty towards the bottom of the *étang*, and the overflow leat tumbled into the main stream, clean and sparkling towards where the boundary between his property and Jacques was blurred and untidy.

Simon was pleased to see that no-one appeared to be around the shack and recalled what Émilie had told him about someone creeping about outside a few nights back. He hated the thought of her alone in the cottage with this apparent madman living next door, and the police *still* hadn't found any evidence against him! At least he'd kept his distance. Simon clenched his fists at the thought of what he'd do to him if he went anywhere *near* Émilie. He dismissed the unpleasant thought. Not today. Today he would *not* entertain uneasy thoughts. He was home and all looked good. A shout came from the *Salamandre*, and he turned to see Henri and Marie beckoning him over. At the table on the terrace sat Philippe, Josiane, Georges and Émilie. What a welcome home they were giving him, he thought happily and without a second thought he walked up the *chemin* and joined them.

***

The bar was packed with tourists many of whom, when they had finished dining began to walk towards the *moulin* to admire the renovations. Georges grunted and pointed, 'I have placed a *propriété privée* sign at the entrance, or you will have no peace!' he said. 'Of course, when the renovations are complete you will be able to charge them for the privilege of looking around, that will be acceptable, *n'est pas?*' He slapped Simon on the back, pleased to welcome back the hard-working businessman.

The friends ordered their food and sat in amiable silence whilst they ate, interrupting to comment on the food or to ask for more bread. At the end of the meal, following the cheese and the coffee, Georges stood to raise his glass.

'We are sorry you had to leave and the village commiserates with you on the loss of your father. This is a hard blow to bear, but you are not alone my friend. You have now returned to your home here in St Honoré, and we are glad. We welcome you back, Simon.'

The friends clapped, and some other couples at other tables, evidently locals and listening to the *maire's* impromptu speech, also clapped. Georges ordered *eau de vie* for them all, except Simon, who politely declined the firewater (there were *some* French gastronomic delights that he didn't really enjoy); and they sat on the terrace watching the sun turn the stones of the old mill building a pretty ochre, glowing warmly. The fierce heat of the day was now thankfully dissipating, and it was time to relax and enjoy the sight of the pretty *moulin*, with its *étang* and backdrop of meadow and trees. To Simon, the French countryside had never looked prettier; and unlike the tourists, he could enjoy it every day. It may change with the seasons, but whether it was in sunshine like today or with a hard frost or snow and a curl of smoke rising from the chimneys, he knew he could be happy here for the rest of his life. He looked around at the faces of his friends here this evening, and with a swelling heart, thought himself very lucky. Under the table he kicked off his sandals and relaxed.

***

Another bottle of *rosé* was ordered and gentle small-talk filled the air before the friends eventually drifted away; firstly Georges had to return home, and then Philippe and Josiane, as it was getting near to Philippe's bed time, Josiane announced to much laughter. Simon and Émilie sat nursing their wine.

'I love the lavender and the geraniums,' Simon said by way of thanks, 'they were a nice surprise. And I see Jojo has got his sheep in.'

'It has been nice to see positive changes, yes.' Émilie agreed,

'But it is back to work tomorrow. The excavator man is arriving at eight, so we will have an early night, I think.'

He looked at her with a twinkle in his eyes.

'Yes *we.*' she responded with a hint of a wicked smile, rubbing her bare foot up his shin. With no more prompting required, Simon paid the bill and the couple walked back to the mill, hand in hand.

***

From his viewpoint, in the bushes next to the *vannes* at their joint boundary Jacques was positively seething. So, *he* was back! The big romance was on-going and from the activity he'd seen in the last few days nothing had changed. He was alarmed to see machinery being moved and realised when he saw the arrival of the large new septic tank that they were continuing with renovations. He'd also seen Philippe raise the leat *vanne* to hold back the water in the shrinking *étang* and empty the wheel pit. Now that they'd finished in the cottage and had basically sorted the main structure of the mill building, there was only the barn remaining. His time was running out! He'd tried to have a closer look the other night, but that damned Fournier woman's dog had heard something as he crept towards the barn. He'd need to wait till she wasn't there, but time was running out!

He crept back to his own cottage and the plastic chair he had positioned to get a good view of the cottage. He'd broken a few branches of elder that obscured his view and they lay reeking of the sour, cemetery smell they exuded. Taking his packet of cigarettes he sat and screwed a new one into the corner of his mouth, under his long, pomaded moustaches, and waited and watched.

***

Morning came and Simon opened his eyes and stretched out his hand. She was gone. He sighed; he'd have to get used to this; her getting up at the crack of dawn, but he was proud of

170

her, managing a bakery on her own. Perhaps when the mill restoration was complete he could help her, but that was at least another year away. First, they'd need to wait for the new wheel and some of the old guys from the Federation would come and with the aid of old photographs and fading recollection they'd fit the myriad of belts and pulleys to the machinery. Philippe offered to redress the existing mill stones, which they'd found round the back of the old shed, and then they'd need to find someone capable of running the mill itself. Maybe they'd be finished in two years, he sighed. Meanwhile, Émilie would run her *boulangerie* from the ground floor. That, at least would be up and running pretty soon. She'd also suggested creating a bedroom with en-suite in the upper floor of the mill, separated off from the dusty granary area at the rear of the buildings, allowing them to rent out the two bedroom cottage as a holiday let; which she felt would be extremely popular and help stop the haemorrhaging of money from Simon's bank account. Now that was an idea he *really* liked, although he could envision the architect throwing all his toys out of the pram at the idea!

***

His thoughts were interrupted as the love of his life appeared with a bang downstairs, announcing breakfast. He dressed quickly and ran down to find her heading back out of the door,

'Have to go, very busy! See you here for lunch at one o'clock.' She threw him a kiss and was gone. Where she got her energy from he'd never know. As he munched almond croissants the men began to arrive, and the air was filled with the sound of the arrival of the excavator driving down the *chemin.* He downed his coffee and went to join them.

At eight the temperature had already reached 30 degrees, and the excavator driver was keen to get on. He positioned the machine at the rear of the mill building and with the precision of a surgeon began to dig out the soil, and fill the skip. Claude was supervising, so Simon joined the others at the wheel pit.

171

The excavator operator had also brought a small bucket to dig this narrow space out, but the workmen were shaking their heads.

'It's too narrow and should be dug out by hand', one said, staring into the narrow pit. Simon was nervous. The last thing they needed was to damage the walls of the pit. He'd previously noticed what looked like a few loose bricks in the walls on one side, but the operator had assured him it would be fine. The skip was full of the excavated soil, but the pit mud and sludge was to be spread on the soil next to the small orchard, where Émilie had said would be good to develop the future vegetable garden.

Less than ten minutes later, the operator was exchanging the buckets and the excavator trundled slowly round to the side of the mill, stretching slowly and delicately into the wheel pit.

Everyone had stopped work to watch. One bucket full slowly came up and was dumped, dripping and stinking next to the orchard, then a second. The pit was deep and it was a full five buckets before the scraping noise alerted them they'd reached the bottom. Then, the relieved operator carefully trundled the machine away to the *chemin* and turned it off. He clambered into the pit to check for any damage and then triumphantly shouted and waved his hand.

The men cheered and Simon pushed past them to see what the commotion was. In his filthy hand gleamed something shiny.

'A Napoleon!' the man whooped loudly, handing the gold coin to Simon, 'What a find!'

He got on his hands and knees in the filthy pit, checking for any more, and emerged crestfallen, 'only one!' he announced, but *what* luck!'

Simon took the coin into the cottage and washed it carefully under the kitchen tap. You could clearly see the head of Napoleon with his laurel wreath on it! The date was 1810, not that far back in history, but still; a gold coin! He was amazed and elated – a gold coin from the reign of the Emperor. They'd need to keep this for a display in the mill. He took some photographs with his phone and then popped the coin into the drawer of the table in the living room. He couldn't wait to show Émilie, but would need to wait another couple of hours, till she finished in the *boulangerie*.

The men stopped work and it was decided that to calm everyone down they'd have a coffee at the *Salamandre*. The excavator driver washed down his machine and trundled back up the *chemin* to his low-loader and waved goodbye as he passed the bar. What a morning!

Back at the mill, the men eventually got back to work. Simon got the key to the *vanne* and slowly let some water from the *étang* out to swill the remaining dirt from the cobbles in the wheel pit. After about five minutes, he raised the *vanne* again. The *étang* was already low and there was no rain forecast for at least ten days. He had to conserve as much water in the pond as possible as he would need to start watering the new fruit trees, and pumping from the *étang* was cheaper than using tap water. A small flow was allowed to escape down the leat that ran down past Jacques property and then on towards the Dordogne. The men frantically scanned the escaping water for any further glint of gold, but they were disappointed.

Arrangements were made for the inspector from SPANC to come and give permission for the new tank to be connected up to the foul water pipes, and then Simon took the coin and went to visit first Émilie then Georges at the *mairie*. A find like this would no doubt have to be reported, and loads of forms completed he assumed.

Georges was delighted and then immediately frowned. Simon and Émilie stood in front of him perplexed.

'I will of course, have to report it; but sadly there was an amendment to the civil code regarding finding treasure just in 2016. I will talk to someone at Périgueux and find out *discreetly* what we do next.' He handed the coin back to Simon, 'Enjoy it today; take photographs, and the legal people might come back to me tomorrow. One coin can't be a big issue, surely. It was only minted in 1810. It's not as if it is ancient.'

Simon was crestfallen, 'You mean the state might *keep* it? Even though it was found on my property?'

Georges nodded sadly. 'I know; the sale would have helped you with the work. Let us hope they come back with a sensible answer.'

Émilie dragged him away and closed the *boulangerie* early. She picked up her wicker basket and calling Eloise, they walked back to the mill for lunch. The men were heading to the *Salamandre,* whilst Émilie cut up the hot quiche she'd made that morning and shared out the salad. They ate hungrily and sipped elderflower cordial with ice.

'What are we doing this afternoon?' she asked.

'Laundry, I'm afraid. And then later watering the fruit trees. It has to be done.'

She nodded, 'I shall start to make some tomato soup to freeze. I have too many tomatoes and cannot use them all so quickly. So, I'll collect what I need and make it here if you like?'

Domestic bliss, he thought happily. She was coming round to the idea, he thought, and then she added, 'And then later this evening I'm going back to my own house. My mother is coming tomorrow evening and I have to tidy-up. *C'est la vie.*'

His face fell, but he shrugged it off valiantly, 'No problem, I understand. So we'll play house this afternoon then. Good.' He smiled lopsidedly as she kissed his cheek and then took the dirty plates to the kitchen before heading back up the *chemin* to collect her soup-making things.

He watched after her for a moment, and then went inside to gather up the clothes that needed washed. He might have a gold coin in his pocket, but he was still his own servant and loaded the first bundle of clothes into the washing machine.

Jacques stood hiding beneath the elder trees seething. Something had happened! He was unsure what but they all seemed very happy and excited about something. He decided to follow the workmen to the bar to find out more. Skulking at the door underneath the balcony terrace he listened in horror and anger as they bragged about their discovery. A gold Napoleon! There *had* to be more. This was *it*. This was the *proof* he'd waited for all those years. He knew old Renauld had told him the truth! The coin could have just fallen into the wheel pit from the mill. All he had to do was get in there and *take* it. He'd have to search around the axle and the wall where it went through. How? *How?* With the Englishman now living there and the girl almost *always* there with her stupid little dog, how could he get in?

He looked over towards the mill. *The hoist opening*. If he could climb onto the low barn roof and then, *somehow* get over to the hoist opening, he could get into the mill. *When* though? It would need to be soon, or *he* would find it! Jacques eyes gleamed. *That must never happen*. If he was discovered he'd have to deal with him; even if it meant killing him with his bare hands. He looked down at his paint-stained hands. Red paint. He'd been painting a naked woman with a gory red slash of a smile. On his hands the red paint looked like blood. His mouth twisted into a fiendish grimace; but blood was *so* much easier to wash off than paint! A strange, high pitched giggle escaped and he quickly covered his mouth lest he was discovered. With his heart pounding excitedly, he looked over at the mill again, his feverish mind working so fast to find a solution. The stash *must* be in the wall near to the wheel axle; how else could the coin have fallen into the wheel pit? Sweat beaded his chin and he wiped it away. He'd have to think this through, and watch to see when they were out. During the day was no good, too many workmen, too many prying eyes. *Night* was the answer, and a night when the girl and her stupid dog were not there. He rubbed his hands together gleefully, and reached for a *Gaulois*. They'd done him a favour really, he grinned to himself; *confirming* the location. All he had to do now was go and collect it.

Chapter 18

Eloise was taking full advantage of her new status as guard dog at the cottage. From the initial night she had slept with Émilie on the bed, she'd taken this as tacit approval, and it had unfortunately become a regular event. Simon wasn't keen on having a dog on the bed, but welcomed her sharp hearing and the small growls she made through the night, when he leaped alert and anxious to put the lights on and explore outside.

Ridiculous, he said to himself. He was getting as jumpy as an old woman. Still, it was good to have the little watch dog there, he said as he climbed wearily back into bed, wondering if she was actually barking and growling just to maintain her continued access to the bed.

***

The police, having stirred up no new evidence and being pushed to move the case onwards, decided that they now had no option but to interview Jacques, and on the Friday morning, they arrived and took him to St Cyprien to the police station, where two detectives were waiting with a bulging folder to begin questioning him.

Georges had been informed as a matter of courtesy and asked to accompany the scenes of crime officers as they took the opportunity to search the shack.

One of them thanked God he was wearing a paper suit as he didn't want to take any fleas home with him, and he handed Georges some elastic bands to secure his trouser bottoms.

'To keep fleas out; but also in case of rats,' he laughed. 'If we disturb any they will look for a dark place to hide, and trouser legs are a favourite.'

Georges hurriedly took a step backwards and stood outside the filthy hovel and refused to go back in. Even so, his eyes were darting everywhere on the rubbish strewn undergrowth outside. He stood fidgeting whilst the officers searched the bedroom, the toilet and then the kitchen.

'*Merde*! Who *lives* like this nowadays?' one officer spat with a shudder as he opened the door of the filthy old cooker. An overflowing cupboard under the old white sink revealed a half used box of latex gloves, which were removed and placed into an exhibits bag. Despite thoroughly searching, it was all they found. No traces of mushrooms, no chemicals, nothing else to build a case. They radioed back to base to let them know, and then left.

***

In St Cyprien Jacques sat quietly in the interview room, saying as little as possible. Previous experience had taught him that the less you said, the less they could catch you out on and he was careful not to incriminate himself. To the questions of the night of the fête he confirmed he was there for a short time. It was *his* village, and everyone from the village was there. But he emphatically denied being close to the table where both Barrie Curtis and Simon Parker had been sitting and eating. He'd sat on the wall, drinking his own wine (which was true); he didn't buy any food as the stallholders were too expensive for him (which was also true) and no, he didn't see anything suspicious (which was partly true).

The lead detective tried a different approach.

'Are you racist, Mr Bordes?' he asked.

The question threw Jacques completely, 'What do you mean?'

'Well, how do you feel about all these foreigners coming to the country? The Senegalese and Tunisians, for example. Many

French patriots think it wrong for us to burden the country with them.'

'I *always* vote for the parties that want to expel them! There's nothing wrong with that! Far too many foreigners that we law-abiding tax payers have to support!' Jacques spat.

The detective knew from his records that Mr Bordes was far from law-abiding and indeed was not honestly declaring his income from the paintings he did sell. He might pass on the tax evasion information to another department, but that was a different matter than the one he was investigating today and he needed to concentrate on the fish he was trying to hook.

'And thank God now that the British have finally left the European Union; it is much harder for them now to come and enjoy the benefits of our country.'

'Not hard enough!' Jacques was warming to the theme now, in spite of himself, 'Coming over here in their *thousands*, buying our homes and forcing the prices up!' He suddenly stopped realising he'd said too much and taking a deep breath added, 'Of course, I'm sure they pay the authorities what is due, and they perhaps employ local people, like the Englishman who bought the old *moulin*.'

'Ah yes; the old mill.' The detective took a sheet of paper out from the rear of the file and read it to himself, 'I see from the *notaire* that *you* made enquiries about buying the mill yourself not too long ago.'

Jacques swallowed, 'Well, not *serious* enquiries. It's just; well, it *is* next door to my property. I was curious. How could a man like me, *with no income* possibly afford to buy a place like that?'

That would show them, he smirked. Trying to trap him. As if he'd fall for that! He was far too clever for that!

'But a ruin like that – well, almost a ruin. Why would you want to even *consider* buying such a place? Were you ever a miller?'

'No! That is peasant work! I am an artiste!' he protested

wildly and then closed his mouth quickly, and reached for his Gauloise, screwing one into his mouth.

The detective probed a little deeper. 'Ah yes, the English seem to have money falling from their pockets, don't they? And the Americans; they also. Coming here and buying everything, gobbling up houses that we French can't afford.'

He reached inside the folder again and pulled out a statement, 'In fact, Mr Bordes, I have a statement here from some Americans who bought a painting from you just a few days ago for 300 euros. Well, that's *some* painting, if I may say so. The buyer said the style reminded her strongly of the artist Salvador Dali.'

Jacques beamed with joy, his eyes gleaming as he visibly puffed with pride. His fingers rose to his moustaches and he smoothed them to the tips, 'Well, *she* had good taste, and admired it so much, I would have been *stupid* to refuse to sell at that price…the price *she offered*. But it was a one-off. I paint to please myself, to emulate the great Dali.'

He babbled on about what a great artist Dali was, how he was working through the body of Jacques Bordes, how lately he felt inspired by him to transcend the life he was living to *become* more like Dali. Then he stopped, panting slightly, eyes wild with fire. He had said too much; his vanity stroked by this *flic*.

The detective stared at the man for some moments before quietly putting the statement away and then continued with the interrogation.

'So, we can see that you are an accomplished painter, in the style of Dali, but what about these foreigners? Eh? This summer we expect a record number of American tourists. If you continue to sell your work and become famous as the *new* Dali, you could then perhaps buy the mill from the Englishman?'

Jacques heart was beating a little too fast. 'I'm no longer interested in the mill,' he growled.

'Oh but surely, that's not true, is it? We have witnesses who will testify that you have in the past *frequently* said you wanted to buy the mill; that you have been seen countless times in and around the mill. That the previous owner, the late Mr Renauld told you some ridiculous story that he'd hidden some gold there.'

'That's *not* a story! It's true!' he yelled in response. Spittle flew from his mouth, and he raised a shaky hand to wipe it away.

'And we have other witnesses to say that you followed the workmen from the mill to the *Salamandre* bar only two days ago, when they discovered a gold coin in the wheel pit of the mill.'

'So?' he folded his arms. As far as he was concerned he was done talking. They couldn't *make* him talk.

The detective saw that he wasn't going to get anywhere further on this line of enquiry, and having nothing further he wished to air at this time he concluded the interview.

'So, Mr Bordes; It looks like you were correct about the gold. It can only be a matter of time now before more is found, I believe. That's going to be some haul for an Englishman.'

He closed the folder and tapped all the papers inside on the table gently to neaten them and stood up.

'Thank you for your time, monsieur. We may need to speak to you again, but that's all for now.'

Jacques was perplexed, 'That's all? You don't want to ask me any questions about anything else?'

'Should we?' The detective looked down at the wretch of a man. His time would come; he was sure of it.

'No, no.'

***

Out in the street in the brassy sunlight, Jacques was sweating profusely. They had nothing; *nothing*. No evidence, no witnesses, nothing. He crossed the road to the cheapest bar in town and ordered a large *pastis,* and sat quietly; going over and over the interview. In fact, he hadn't told them anything, really. Okay, so he'd sold a painting; *big deal*. He'd been at the fête, so had *everyone*. The *flics* hadn't once asked him anything about the pizza, about the car…nothing. Unconnected. No motive, no evidence, no witnesses! He congratulated himself on being superiorly clever, and then ordered another *pastis*.

And they knew about the gold. *Only a matter of time before more is found*, he'd said; that detective. That was evident; time was of the essence and the Englishman was a fool if he was not already looking for it.

'*Not if I find it first!*' he answered himself out loud, banging the empty glass on the table and walking away. The sooner he could get back to the village, the better.

The two plain-clothes men sitting at the far end of the bar walked back across to the detective's office in the police station.

'I owe you ten euros!' one said to the chief detective, 'You were right! I think we have the fish on the hook now! He sat for a few minutes looking confused and worried and then – a transformation! You must have *said* something.'

'*Of course*. To catch a big fish you just need the right bait. But we need to watch him carefully now; round the clock. He will try again; soon. And that means the Englishman is in danger.'

***

Back eventually at his home, Jacques immediately realised the house had been searched. That was, of course, no surprise. That was probably why they let him go – no evidence! His confidence was overflowing as he took another fresh canvas and settled it on the easel. What would Dali paint today? He always painted things he loved, so Jacques carried the easel through the elder trees and set it up with the view of the mill. A landscape with the moulin as the main subject. That way he could create *and* watch the Englishman. He immediately began to squeeze tubes of paint onto his palette and readied himself. A light touch of charcoal to mark out the subject and when he was happy with the mill and *étang* on the canvass he began.

***

Émilie's mother had arrived and whilst her daughter attended to the shop and customers, she cleaned the apartment upstairs. After the lunch rush Émilie joined her and the two planned their brief time together, whilst chatting about the sale of the building. The news had only come via a telephone call from her lawyer that morning – the people who wanted to buy the building had put in an attractive offer and the errant husband was keen to accept on his part.

'He's obviously keen for both some cash and for the divorce to proceed,' her lawyer mentioned dryly on the 'phone.

Émilie agreed to the sale, her mother eavesdropping as concerned mothers do. She pursed her lips, waiting for the opportunity to advise at the end of the telephone call.

'Don't tell *anyone* until it's all in writing.'

'Mother, I *know* what I'm doing.'

'Humph. When am I to meet this Anglo-Saxon of yours then? I suppose he is going to come for dinner? What are we cooking?'

'Tonight, and he will collect us in his car and we will be going out for dinner to the Auberge at Le Moustier. And you *will* be nice, mother. He's nice and his French is improving every day.'

Like most mothers, Danielle Lambert wanted only the best for her daughter. She'd never liked that scoundrel she'd married; he was far too smooth and expensive. One could *never* trust a handsome man. Hopefully the failure of the marriage and the experience of life living alone had finally taught her daughter that life was hard and fairy-tale romances were just for children's books. She herself would have to look her elegant best this evening to scrutinise and intimidate the suitor. The Auberge, eh? Well, at least he had *taste*!

In the afternoon, the ladies walked Eloise down the *chemin* to the mill and met Simon supervising the connection of the pipes for the new *fosse*. Not the most glamorous of jobs, her mother whispered, twitching her nose.

'There is *no* smell, mother. It's all brand new!' Émilie rolled her eyes, 'Come, say hello to Simon.'

Simon straightened up to meet the frosty-looking matriarch and bowed slightly. '*Enchanté madame*,' he smiled, and in French asked to be excused his appearance and dirty hands, 'Would you like to see the progress inside, and where Émilie's new *boulangerie* will be?'

Madame graciously nodded and smiled, and as Simon led the way, she raised her eyebrows with a smile at her daughter, 'Well, he has manners anyway.'

Émilie took her by the hand and squeezed a warning, 'Be *nice*, Maman.'

The next half hour was spent with both Simon and Émilie explaining how things would look when complete; then Émilie showed her mother the small cottage.

'And you will be moving in here, I assume?' her mother said archly in French.

Émilie was horrified, 'There are *two* bedrooms, maman; but yes; until a bedroom can be made in the mill and we can let the cottage for holidays, then this is where I will live.'

Simon could feel the tension, and took the opportunity to lay his case,

'Madame, your daughter has not had an easy time in the last few years. Her husband has deserted her and she has courageously run a physically tiring business on her own. This is to her credit. *However*; you *do not*, I think want to see your daughter unhappy. She deserves some comfort in life and a nicer place to live than an apartment above a shop. Forgive me Émilie, but it is true.'

Madame was charmed! He understood *perfectly*! Perhaps he *was* a good find, she mused.

Simon, seeing no objection, continued, 'I am financially able to complete this project and am the sole heir to my late father's estate. Whilst Émilie and I are only just becoming acquainted with each other, we are sensible and taking our time. After all, (and here he regurgitated something Jojo, the great romantic had said earlier) one does not immediately buy a pair of shoes without trying them on to ensure they are a good fit.'

Madame's face was a picture of shock and indignation.

'What I *mean* Madame; if you will excuse my poor French, is that Émilie must be allowed to see if I am suitable for *her*. I am *completely* assured that she is more than suitable for me.'

With a beaming smile Danielle Lambert kissed him on both cheeks, to the delight (and relief) of the two young people. Simon, feeling he'd best not to spoil the moment, begged to return to the unfortunate duty of supervising the workmen, and the two ladies returned to the village.

'What a dragon!' Jojo said with awe from the safety of the mill.

'She *is* terrifying!' Simon laughed.

'To see what your wife will become, look at the mother.' Claude warned with a wagging finger, and they all returned to the *fosse* and the comparatively easy job of connecting pipes.

***

The day passed without further incident and later that evening Simon was charm personified as he took the two ladies to dinner and Émilie explained that she had now accepted the offer on the *boulangerie* building and that the sale was now in progress. Simon ordered champagne and toasted the women, with the ambiguous toast of 'new beginnings.' Madame's eyes twinkled as she sipped the champagne. This man might be *exactly* what Émilie needed. He was educated, charming, had money and expectations, and yes, he was *quite* good looking.

That of course was the cherry on the cake; not essential, but certainly an added inducement. She watched as they chatted at ease with each other, and as the pretty young waitress served them, she was pleased to note that Simon only had eyes for her daughter. She enquired why he had chosen the mill project in the first place, and he explained about his own marriage and the need to now start somewhere fresh. Now he was *very* happy living in the village; the mill would not be completed quickly and he did not need to move onto a new project. He was lucky, he explained, that not only had he fallen in love with a beautiful and sensible girl, but he had fallen in love with French rural life and intended to stay and make it home. His only sadness was that his father hadn't met Émilie, and hadn't lived to see the mill. Madame would understand the importance of family, of course.

Madame did indeed, and relaxed into his company. Yes, he would do *very* well indeed.

***

The next morning Danielle Lambert decided to take the train back home to Toulouse, and Émilie arranged for Simon to take her to the station. He courteously held the passenger door open for her, and closed it gently.

As they drove she casually mentioned that she had heard about the poisoning and that Émilie had reluctantly told her about the other incidents that had taken place.

'I hope that all this stops now. I don't want to think that Émilie could be in any danger living at the mill. It would be good if the police got on with arresting this lunatic.'

Simon nodded and sighed, changing gear.

'The problem is the lack of evidence, it seems. I'm hoping he's had a good fright and that this is the end of it. Apparently the police had him in for questioning, but then let him go again. The detective called me saying that although they have a motive, there are no corroborating witnesses and very little evidence. The poor chap who actually ate the pizza has now had a liver transplant, and although still very poorly, is expected to make a recovery.'

He turned and stared hard at Danielle, 'I'd never put your daughter into any danger. And anyhow, we have the best little guard dog around, you know.'

Danielle Lambert didn't smile back. A man who can try to poison someone for money would have no scruples poisoning a dog, she thought grimly.

Chapter 19

Barrie Curtis was dead.

It was the talk of the village, and shortly after he had been officially informed, Georges had made an emergency visit to the health centre and demanded anti-depressants and tranquillisers from his doctor. His nerves were in *shreds*, but the official duties of his position demanded he fulfil his obligations and not just retire to his bed, which he fervently wished to. After making the agonising (for them both) visit to Sue Curtis with his deputy he drove straight to the Chief of Police in St Cyprien; and the loud and very angry discussion that followed could be heard in the street and the little bar opposite. He did not get the answers he was looking for, and stormed out, indignant and anxious.

When he returned to his little commune van Georges gripped the steering wheel tightly, banging his sweating head on it again and again. Why his village? *Why?* This was not Paris or Marseilles for God's sake! It was a tiny village where nothing happened for generations. Now the TV people would arrive *en-masse again*, bringing the wrong kind of publicity and *still* the police seemed unwilling to do anything. No arrests, no conclusion. What were they *waiting* for? And now a funeral had to be organised; and the widow distraught, stating she would return to England as soon as possible. St Honoré didn't need *that sort* of publicity! Georges mopped his brow. He needed to calm down. The last thing he needed was a heart attack on top of everything else. He had so much to do and not enough hours in the day; and his wife was forever telling him to retire and let someone else become *maire*.

He rolled down the windows of the van and took some slow calming breaths. After a moment or two he then raised his eyes in silent prayer and began the short drive back to the village that was currently the most famous in France for all the wrong reasons.

***

The St Honoré bush telegraph had already alerted Émilie of the terrible news almost as soon as she had opened, and she had quickly shut the shop, placing a paper sign in the window to say she would be open today only between eight and nine. Then she ran down to the mill. Simon was upstairs working on the first floor grain floor and immediately sensed something was wrong, and rushed down to meet her. She dragged him into the privacy of the cottage and blurted out the devastating news. Almost an instant later, Simon's mobile rang. It was the Chief of Police at St Cyprien. They were now officially investigating a murder, and would be re-interviewing all the witnesses as a matter of course. They would arrange a *rendezvous* with him in due time to try and see if they could add anything to his statement.

He rubbed his hand over his eyes when they had rung off. Was there ever a day in this village when nothing extraordinary happened? What happened to the peace and quiet of the countryside he'd moved here for? Living in St Honoré was like living in a soap opera.

'*Simon*; I will be back here at nine,' Émilie interrupted his thoughts. 'The TV crews will descend on the village like flies, so we will go away for the day. I must go back now. The *boulangerie* will be full of people gossiping. Vultures! That *poor* woman! They are saying that after the funeral here she will take Barrie's ashes and return to the UK. After living here for many years, the house will be sold and she wants nothing to do with France ever again!'

'I don't understand. I thought he was on the mend? Everyone

189

said so; you, the police, the *maire*. He'd had a liver transplant and was doing okay?'

Émilie shook her head, 'It was all very sudden. His body rejected the new organ and the toxins were too much for an older person already badly poisoned. He died late last night.'

She looked at him with tears in her eyes, 'That could have been *you*. Or *me*. Or both of us. I'm *frightened* Simon. That maniac will stop at nothing, and the police don't seem to have enough on him to make an arrest.'

Simon took her by the shoulders, 'Right, you're *not* staying alone in that bakery. You bring your stuff down later today and bring Eloise. At least we'll be together and Eloise will warn us if anyone is around. Although, I'd imagine now that this is a murder enquiry our *friend* next door will not be at liberty for long.'

He sent her off and explained to Jojo and Claude that due to the change of circumstances he'd be away for most of the day, 'You can get me on my mobile, but if the TV crews are to come, I don't want to be here.'

'We've heard – my wife sent me a text message. Shocking – a murder in the village, and the man everyone thinks is the murderer living here too! Don't worry, I expect the police to come and arrest that lunatic any time today. But we will keep watch.'

At lunchtime the usual black-edged funeral announcement was posted on the church door and at the board next to the cemetery; confirming the death of Mr Barrie Curtis, the service at the church and then the cremation at Les Eyzies, in just three days time.

Georges arrived back to find that his helpful secretary had organised a suitable floral arrangement and card of condolence to be sent to the Curtis house. He nodded his thanks and retreated to his office. The desk was littered with telephone messages, and the secretary came in unbidden with a pot of coffee and biscuits. He stared at her with surprise and disgust.

Biscuits? What the hell was this? She shrugged her shoulders in apology; 'the *boulangerie* was closed when I went. The sign on the door says they will reopen for an hour.'

His telephone almost immediately rang, and he began the long process of fielding TV stations questions, the polite but clipped enquiry from his superiors at Périgueux, and many calls from village residents demanding to know what *he* and the police were doing about this situation. He dealt with about a dozen phone calls and then left; telling his secretary he was going to visit the widow again and then would be at home for the rest of the day. She was to tell *no-one*.

***

Sue Curtis was distraught. She allowed Georges into the house and through the fog of cigarette smoke to the sitting room. On the coffee table next to the overflowing ashtray was a glass of wine, which she emptied and refilled, whilst Georges again offered to help in making any arrangements. She shook her head; her son was on his way to the airport and would be with her by dinner time. The undertakers had been and collected Barrie and he was at their premises now and she would go and sit with him until her son arrived. *Why* did they have to organise the funeral so quickly? She hadn't even had time to get used to the idea, and it would be impossible for any relations to have time to organise to attend? Georges shrugged his shoulders and explained that this is the procedure in France. She was furious and in anger and hurt lashed out. She had already contacted an *immobilier*, she told him with her red-rimmed eyes blazing.

Poor Georges was only trying to help, but hampered both by the widow's failure to fully understand the cultural differences between England and France, and her understandable anger. He tried again; explaining that although he understood her grief at her beloved husband's sudden death after the ...*incident;* perhaps she needed to take time to think; perhaps discuss with her son before making a rash decision to leave the village she had lived in for many years.

Sue Curtis was having none of it. She would see the funeral out and return to her family; the house *would* be sold and she would try and forget the whole horrible episode. She then rounded on Georges, demanding to know *why* he had done so little; *why* the police had not arrested anyone yet; *why* was her poor husband killed by someone the whole community *knew* to be the murderer.

Georges had no answers for her, and after repeating his sincere condolences returned home and hid under the covers of his bed.

***

Émilie and Simon left the village, the streets filled with TV crews and reporters attempting to interview everyone and anyone. The villagers were scandalised and shut their doors in their faces. The official police response was to deploy *gendarmes* around the village; at the Curtis house, outside the mill and at the *mairie*. Unofficially, behind the scenes, there was a great deal of investigation still going on; mainly leading to dead ends and pointing to a complete lack of evidence.

The couple drove at speed out towards St Cyprien, passing Police Headquarters, under siege by more TV vans, and soon were on the road towards Beynac. Outside Police Headquarters tempers were frayed and the Chief of Police, standing on the steps, stretched out his hands and tried to calm the public *and* answer the questions of the Press without actually telling them anything. The investigation had reached an important point, he said; some new information had come to light, which was being investigated at this very minute, he said; they must be patient…

***

Jacques was pacing up and down and round and round his studio. He couldn't paint in the dark; having had to lock the door and pull the curtains in his home. Reporters had been banging on his door all morning, there were police *everywhere* and no time or space to think or work. He couldn't even get out to buy bread, and had no food in the house! To fill his empty stomach and calm his nerves he drank. At nine o'clock in the morning he had almost finished a bottle of red wine, trying to dull the racing, jumbled thoughts in his head. Over and over again, the same thoughts running around and around his head; tormenting him; *accusing* him. He'd *killed* a man. He should go to church and confess, and at least he would get peace and his head would stop hurting him.

Confess what? That he'd killed the wrong man?

His dwindling conscience was under assault and beaten back by a stronger voice in his head. Confess? *Why* should he confess? He'd be a *fool* to say anything now, when he was *so close*. The police had *nothing* or they would have arrested him by now. He was in the clear and needed to find some courage, the voice in his head said.

Jacques thought this was an excellent idea and opened a new bottle of wine, shakily pouring himself a tumbler full of courage, and downed it immediately. More thumping on his door. He moaned quietly, rocking back and forward on his chair as he sat in the dark, pretending the house was empty. Alone with the tormentors in his head he reflected on his life; chewing the ends of his long moustaches. Once he'd found the cache of gold he'd *leave* this wretched village. There was nothing and no-one here for him, no reason to stay. He would take the gold and leave; move to the south of France, where he would be free to paint; where he could sell his Dali-esque paintings to rich Americans; where he could *be* Dali. All he needed to do was get his hands on that gold. It was sitting there – *waiting* for him; sitting in the mill wall near the opening where the wheel axle came out of the mill. Beckoning to him night and day, *teasing* him. *It was his for the taking!*

He squeezed his hands around his head tightly, trying to

stop the voices in his head. The quiet whining voice of his conscience eventually gave up; outdone and overpowered by the stronger, louder voice telling him that this was his *due*; that he'd come *so far* now; that it was *easy*. That he needed to act *now*.

***

Whilst Simon and Émilie walked around Beynac, trying to distance themselves from the mêlée in St Honoré, and Jacques went quietly and completely mad in his house; plans were underway at the Police Station. At the briefing in the Chief's office, the men were informed of their duties. All leave was cancelled, and they would work 12 hour shifts until this case was concluded, but the Chief didn't think it would take long. Today, *every* witness was to be re-interviewed; plain clothes men were doubled-up to walk around the village day and night; and *must* keep their ears and eyes open. The Chief felt that the news of Monsieur Curtis's death would be the turning point; would give them something to conclude the case. What that something was he didn't yet know; but he was sure it would be soon. *Something was going to happen.*

***

At Beynac, the tourists trooped around the medieval keep dragging their children with them, oblivious to the couple sitting looking out over the Dordogne. They were quiet, sitting close to each other, holding hands, trying to distance themselves from the sad events of the morning. A swallowtail butterfly landed on some yellow wildflowers nearby and Simon tried to be pleased. He was surrounded by beautiful countryside, sitting in the shadow of a fairytale château with a beautiful girl by his side. He ought to be supremely happy and content; but the swallows and house martins wheeled around the rocky outcrop below them, screaming as they vied for positions in the rocks. It was a jarring note and echoed the discomforting thoughts in his head.

The knowledge that he'd managed a couple of lucky escapes, but that the perpetrator was still at large, and now his girlfriend was also in danger was disturbing. The police *obviously* had no evidence and this meant that although everybody disliked and belittled Jacques Bordes, he'd proved himself to be cunning and as slippery as an eel. The azure sky and blinding sunshine forced him to look down to the restful greens of the valley and the meandering river.

Far below, a *gabare* was cruising up and down the Dordogne, carrying passengers making the most of their holiday in the area. The scene was idyllic and he knew he was lucky to live in such a beautiful and historic region, but still he was troubled. His forehead was beaded with sweat and he felt uncomfortable. The heat was building and far off to the East storm clouds were starting to tower into thunderheads.

'There will be an *orage* tonight,' Émilie murmured, 'it will break this humidity.'

'Good. We need a good downpour. It might get rid of the Press too,' Simon answered crossly.

'Let's go find somewhere to eat,' she suggested, trying to pull him out of himself.

'Just a little longer,' he said. 'It's nice to just sit quietly.'

And so they remained for a while, watching the river below washing the valley clean. They eventually drove home arriving late afternoon and parked outside the *boulangerie*. Simon helped her load the pickup with some clothes and personal items and they returned to the mill with Eloise in tow. The little dog gambolled happily around their feet as they emptied the car, both of them relieved that the reporters seemed to have given up for the day. At Émilie's suggestion, they returned a second time to the *boulangerie* for some of her furniture and carefully transported it back to its new home. Simon was delighted; this indicating that she had indeed made her decision about moving in permanently. The bigger pieces, such as the armoire and the bed could wait. Henri shouted from the *Salamandre* that tonight's special was Provençal Chicken, and they nodded and shouted back that they would be there at seven.

Once washed and changed, the rest of the afternoon was spent sorting a space in the fitted wardrobes for Émilie's clothes, and she happily arranged her cookery books on the bookcase in the living room. The commitment from the girl cheered Simon up immensely. They rearranged the furniture to fit her treasured pieces in, the pair laughing and good-naturedly arguing about the merits of each piece in turn. Just before they left for dinner, he caught her hand and held it to his lips.

'Thank you. It's been a horrible day, but spending it with you has made it bearable.'

She kissed his cheek, stroking his fringe back into place, and raised her eyes to his.

'Is that not right? Are we not to be partners in everything? Good and bad together? I will be here for you when you are sad and things are a burden; and you for me also.'

'Sweet girl, I love you so much. Thank you.'

'I love you too. This is life. Now come on, I'm starving.'

The first fat raindrops started as they ran across the road, and as they sat at their secluded table, the storm broke, with jagged lightning breaking the sky somewhere to the East. The lights flickered in the restaurant and the tourists' *oooh'd* and *aaah'd* at the show the storm put on for them. When they had finished eating and were relaxing with coffee and tiny almond biscuits, the storm appeared at least for the moment, to have exhausted its supply of rain, although the thunder and lightening continued. Now with the humidity broken, the temperature had dropped; and they headed back home to the mill, carefully sidestepping the puddles.

At the door Émilie shivered, and Simon rubbed her shoulder, 'Alright?'

'It's nothing, just a change of temperature,' she smiled brightly, casting an almost imperceptible glance towards the far end of the *etang* and the brooding darkness.

'Don't worry. We have Eloise, the super guard dog, remember?' Simon said more cheerfully than he felt, and they went in, closing and locking the door behind them.

***

The barn owl roosting in the barn, sat watching; twitching his head from side to side. The rain began to fall steadily again, so there would be no hunting in the rain for him tonight, but from his vantage point in the barn hoist opening, his eyes saw everything. Night was his element, and he was superbly adapted for it. He watched the couple returning home; noted the small movements of the two dark figures hidden in the shadows at the corner of the dark *boulangerie;* and was particularly interested in the sounds coming from the shack at the far end of the *étang*. The tumbling of the now swollen stream somewhat disturbed his hearing, but the owl; all-seeing and all-hearing was alert. Someone was quietly but steadily moving along the side of the leat down by the elder trees.

197

Chapter 20

Jacques Bordes had dressed for his part with care and attention. Black trousers, black top and a home-made Zorro-type mask for his face. He topped it off with a black beanie hat, stuck his penknife in his pocket and picked up his small torch. He squinted into the cracked bathroom mirror and seemed pleased with his appearance. After waiting an hour after they had arrived home, the mill was finally in darkness. To his annoyance, he realised the girl was staying. In fact, from the movement that day of her furniture into the mill it looked as if she was going to be a *permanent* fixture there, and that meant the stupid dog would be there too! It *had* to be tonight, he'd decided. He'd seen the increased police presence around the village, and realised he was running out of time; It *must* be tonight. With a final long swig of the nearly empty *third* bottle of red wine, he turned off the lights and ventured out.

It was exhilarating, he thought as he slowly walked through the soaking long grass at the side of the leat. His senses heightened, he heard a 'plop' in the water and identified it as a frog. *Probably* a frog, he thought; a rat would have been almost silent. As his eyes got used to the dark his spirits rose with every step he took towards the mill. The steadily falling rain failed to extinguish his excitement, and the nearer he got the slower and quieter he forced himself to be. He must *not* alert the dog. He had all night, he told himself.

***

At the top of the *chemin* where it joined the main road next to the *boulangerie*, two sodden plain-clothes detectives were now thoroughly fed up. One reached into his pocket for his cigarettes, only to be hissed at.

'You *can't* light up! The Chief said no noise, no lights.'

The other thrust his hands into his pockets angrily, 'This is *ridiculous!* No-one is going to be out in this rain! Anyway, I'm going for a piss round the corner. I can't have a *silent* piss, you know!' he strode off around the corner to relieve himself, and to have a quick smoke out of sight.

The other stood quietly. With years more experience, he knew if the Chief had a hunch, it was normally the right one. But his colleague was right; no-one would be out on a night like this. Still; the Chief was never usually wrong…

***

Jacques had finally made it to the gravelled parking area outside the buildings. His trainers and trousers were sodden and uncomfortable, from walking through the long wet grass. He knew that the gravel would betray him and alert the dog, so he walked very slowly on the grass towards the barn, his heartbeat thumping in his ears. His plan; which he'd been working on all day with the aid of a pair of binoculars, was to climb up the barn roof and drop down to the grain door opening just below the apex. Once inside he would just walk quietly through to the connecting mill and downstairs to where the axle came through the thick wall. Then he could just quietly search around till he found the gold.

With a sudden stop he nearly, so *very* nearly walked into the hay tedder and old cart that were standing outside the barn building. It was so dark in the continuous rain he could barely see his hand in front of his face, but to use the torch now would be stupid. He felt his way gingerly around the old machinery and found the corner of the building.

The barn roof, covered with old-fashioned flat terracotta tiles reached down to about five feet off the ground. How the hell was he going to get onto the roof? he despaired, and then remembered the old barrels. Feeling around he found one, lying; thank God, on its side and therefore not full of water. He quietly rolled it over to the corner and placed it upside down next to the building wall. With some difficulty he managed to finally get on top of the barrel and onto the sloping roof.

Slowly, slowly he inched upwards, through the rivulets of cold water, using the toes of his trainers to grip the slippy surface. He knew the best place to hang down to get into the opening was just under the apex. This was about twenty feet from the ground, but the hoist bar above the opening itself was a mere four feet below the apex. If he lowered himself to the hoist bar, it was simple from then on. Quietly and slowly he inched upwards, along the slope, his body flattened on the soaking tiles. When he thought he was about a third of the way up the roof he stopped to rest. The exertion was exhausting and he was soaking wet. Not having eaten at all he felt a little light-headed, and wished he could light a cigarette. The ridiculous thought and his stretched nerves made him giggle, and he fought to smother the noise. His heart thumped in his chest as he listened, straining his ears to try and pick up any sound that he had disturbed the sleepers within. Nothing.

Again, he inched forwards and felt upwards with his outstretched arm. Not there yet, but he *must* be close. He'd rest at the apex. His fingers were *so* cold now. He had to clench and unclench his fists as he moved slowly, feeling the tiles sucking the heat from him.

A thought suddenly struck him that he was being ridiculously stupid. What was he *doing?* At his age he was climbing a soaking wet roof, *in the dark*, without ropes. Fear shot through him and he clung to the roof unmoving.

He was a coward, a voice in his head mocked. No, he was just *resting*, he answered himself.

If he turned back now, the Englishman would have the gold! Anger and adrenaline coursed through him as he acknowledged that this would be his last chance to locate the gold. The *flic* at St Cyprien had been right. It was only now a matter of time before the Englishman found it. Unless *he* found it first. A flash of lightening filled the sky and for a split-second he saw that he was only a foot or so from the apex. With his bravado rising he reached up and pulled hard on the ridge tile, hauling himself up. *Now* he could rest. And he needed to.

He was icy-cold now and shivering, wet though, and his fingers clumsy and slow. He needed to gather his strength now for the drop to the hoist bar. If he held onto the ridge tiles at the apex and faced the roof he could just reach the bar with his feet, then walk his hands down the stone blocks of the wall and swing himself in. He just needed to steady himself. He was *so* tired. He'd just rest there a moment longer.

Inside, the voices started again. '*Get on with it! You don't have all night, and someone may drive around the corner and that will be you – caught!*'

'You should get down now, before you fall and break your neck,' the too quiet voice of reason suggested.

'*That gold is waiting for you. Waiting!*'

He reached out with his feet and started to lower himself from the apex. There was no going back now, and he prayed that his fingers wouldn't give up. And then, his foot touched the bar. *Joy and relief.* He stretched down and placed one foot on the bar, stretched to his full height, and started to move one arm down to cling onto the stone wall.

'I've *done it*! I'm *there*!' he said in his head, jubilant; brazening out the fear. But the voices continued, as he finally crouched down on the bar, which began to strain. His heart was thumping, trying to leap out of his chest and his ears ringing with his blood pressure mounting. He *had* to swing through the opening as quickly as possible; but suddenly doubted his physical strength. The effort to get this far had exhausted him.

'*Who do you think you are, old man?*' the voice sneered, as Jacques hesitated.

'I'm Dali!' he cried out loud and angry.

And it was then that the barn owl, disturbed by the alien presence and the outcry sailed forwards from the shadow of the barn, and escaped through the opening. The man's foot slipped from the bar and with a ghastly scream he plummeted; flinging scrabbling hands upwards, combing the air with his frantic, searching fingers until he found and gripped the bar with one hand and then the other.

***

At the top of the *chemin* the two detectives leaped into action and turned their torches down towards the mill, picking out the sheets of rain frozen in the beams of light, and very little else. The older one pulled out his radio and called for back-up and then they raced down towards the mill.

Simon leaped out of bed and Eloise was barking her head off from the top of the bed. Pulling his jeans and shoes on quickly Simon ordered Émilie to stay inside, as he raced downstairs and flung the switch for all the outside lights and ran outside.

The rain was now torrential, and for a moment all he could see was the rain caught in the lights. Bolts of rain, like grey spears piercing the ground as far as he could see in the lit-up area around the building. Approaching sirens and two policemen running into the yard. There was noise and confusion everywhere, and they all looked around, beams of light from the torch darting and searching and failing to locate the source of the scream. The thunder, the lightning, the torrential rain, police sirens, the dog barking, the police now shining their torches up at the mill roof. Simon pulled a jacket from inside the door and went out again.

The torches had found their target, and caught in their light, and the flashes of lightening, Jacques was hanging onto the hoist bar by his arms, kicking his legs in an attempt to get his feet back on the hoist bar. He was crying and screaming incoherently, whilst the police were yelling for him to hang on – help was coming. Lights were suddenly popping on all over the village. At the *Salamandre* Henri and Marie roused from their bed had turned on the lights and were watching from the balcony terrace; Philippe had rushed down the *chemin* and gripped Simon's shoulder tightly as he took in the scene.

They stood helpless, staring in horror and disbelief at the man writhing and twisting above them, caught and illuminated by the lightning and torches, he appeared like a tormented dancer caught in disco strobe lights. Then he froze; and everyone in turn held their breath. The air filled with the noise of straining metal; a tearing, wrenching noise. All eyes including Jacques' looked up at the bar, which was slowly but surely pulling itself out of the stone block above the opening.

With a final terrifying scream the hoist bar pulled free from the stone block and Jacques Bordes plummeted earthwards and skewered himself fatally on the tines of the hay tedder.

Simon turned away from horrific spectacle, sick to his stomach. The other onlookers, including the policemen were horrified into silence, and the only sound was the continuous heavy fall of rain and the diluted sound of approaching sirens. Émilie stumbled out of the cottage door in a dressing gown and raised her hand to her mouth, before Simon stood in front of her to block the view.

'Don't look! Go back inside. *It's over*. Émilie; go in, now. '

The girl stared, wide-eyed, nodded silently and went inside, leaving the men outside.

The younger detective walked over to the grass and threw up. His colleague averted his eyes and waited for the Chief to arrive; summoning up enough professionalism to tell everyone to keep back.

Philippe turned to Simon, shook his head in disbelief. He would telephone Georges, he said; and as he trudged back up the chemin, herded a few concerned villagers back to their homes.

The Chief; who had been parked nearby, sped down to the

front of the mill, churning gravel as he skidded to a halt.

He took in the whole situation at a glance, and motioned to the detective, 'Tape, forensics, doctor. Don't bother with an ambulance; he's beyond help.'

He then turned to Simon, 'We will talk inside please.'

Simon led him inside the cottage, where Émilie had boiled water for coffee. She poured a good measure of brandy into three cups and passed them around. The Chief stood dripping on the stone flagged floor and downed the scalding coffee in one.

'You are unharmed?'

When he acknowledged the nods of the couple, he raised a hand to wipe the rain from his face.

'It's over. Now, we will have to wait for lights and forensics, as this is a crime scene now,' he said, staring at his watch. 'It will not be light for three more hours, but I imagine you will not sleep. I have to get a tent up to preserve the area for forensics, but we will talk later.' He grimaced slightly, 'A bad end; but at least we have been spared a trial and you are *safe* Monsieur Parker.'

***

Morning dawned with thick clouds and an ominous silence. Simon and Émilie had spent the remainder of the night cuddled together on the sofa with a blanket, with Eloise sitting guarding them. For once, the girl had not risen to go to her work at the *boulangerie*. Today, they would *not* open. Policemen were still busy outside, with the forensic team trying to trace the deceased's steps from his home to the mill. The weather hampered them considerably, but they had managed to trace his journey through the flattened grass and photograph the scene of death before the rain had washed the bloodstains from the gravel around the tedder. They had erected a white forensics tent over the tedder to give the deceased some dignity from the eyes of the Press and ghoulish on-lookers that had thronged around the *Salamandre,* drinking coffee and eating breakfast, but evidently only there to enjoy the spectacle.

Eventually a white van arrived and the body had been removed, and then the policemen, who had been on duty all night were finally replaced by another shift. Simon and Émilie managed to exit the cottage and went to the *boulangerie* to escape the crime scene. Locking the door behind them, they went upstairs and slept, exhausted by the events of the previous night.

Georges was busy in the *mairie*. He'd summoned the committee and explained the sequence of events as told to him by the Chief of Police. He had already made a brief visit to Madame Curtis to inform her of the incident, and she received the news, not with jubilation, but resignation.

His committee, summoned for an emergency meeting, were now discussing the future of Jacques property and possessions. It was well known that there were no relatives and no friends. The *notaire* confirmed that there was no will, and he would clarify the legal position of the ownership of the building. Meanwhile, another funeral had to be arranged, after the necessary police investigation and medical examination of the body. The *mairie* would pay for a cremation and the ashes disposed of discreetly. The committee agreed that in the circumstances, this would be best.

The officers tasked with searching the shack owned by the deceased found a partly completed canvas on the easel; a dark mill with a forbidding dark pool at its side. Wild tumultuous heavy clouds sat above the mill, punctuated by wild strokes of black and indigo, painted by a tormented and frenzied hand. This was Jacques final painting, and so unlike Dali in style. In fact, there were hints of Van Gogh with swirling, wild dabs of black, blue and violet. There was one small bright area of colour on the canvas. Blink and you might miss it, but where the wheel was attached to the building, there was a smudge of yellow. The forensics team, noting the subject matter thought it may throw some light onto the obsession of the man, and so the painting was removed, wrapped and transported back to Headquarters. The empty wine bottles were bagged for examination, the contents of the room photographed, diaries and paperwork collected, and neatly; oh so neatly and without any emotion, Jacques Bordes life was catalogued and removed.

***

The next few weeks smoothed the turbulence of that decisive night, and the stone that had been thrown into the tranquil pond that was St Honoré had finally settled into small everyday ripples. After the two funerals the notoriety of the village had died down, tourists filled the *gites* and *chambre d'hotes* and the restaurant and the bar at the *Salamandre*. The stormy humid weather had subsided and the village and surrounding countryside reclaimed its golden glow and relaxed appearance.

***

Amongst the humdrum and ordinary, there were some interesting changes afoot. Philippe Cholet had made a big decision. Whilst quietly working on dressing and re-cutting the mill stones, he had been thinking. There is plenty of time for thinking when you are quietly, methodically chiselling rock, he thought. For every action, there is an equal reaction, he remembered, wiping his chisel clean. Here he was now, chiselling mill stones for Simon. He was being paid for the job, despite his insistence that it was a gift; a gesture of their friendship. In exchange, Simon; now in a quiet phase of the building works, whilst he awaited permission to continue with the mill renovations, had offered to update the infamous upstairs bedroom and shower room in the Cholet's house. Josiane was thrilled of course, and Philippe had told her to choose whatever she liked, *within reason*. Philippe would pay for the building materials and Simon would provide the labour. It was an arrangement that suited them both.

When he finished cutting the stones on this, the last day of his final weeks' vacation before Christmas, he had decided to retire. Josiane had been nagging him since the turn of the year, and he felt ready for a change. He was a strong man, but aware of his years; and the events of the last few months had made him retrospective and thoughtful. A long holiday away with his wife might just be the tonic he needed to put the spring back into his step. He had been thinking this since the night of the death of Jacques Bordes. Perhaps getting away from the village, and seeing a wider, more vibrant world out there would help him put things back into perspective. The events of the past few months could not, and indeed *should* not be erased, but he needed to come to terms with them and then move on. Life was hard and short, but he was due a good pension and had had some interesting ideas of taking a new direction in life when he returned refreshed.

***

He straightened his back and blew the granite dust away, admiring the clean deep cuts in the stone. It was a good job and would not have to be redone for many years. Time for a coffee, he thought and walked outside the mill to find Simon. The gravel area was now cleared of machinery; the hay tedder having been finally released by the police and sold to a farmer in the north of the department. The old wooden cart had been repainted and was filled with pots of geraniums, and made an attractive feature between the orchard and the parking area.

The workmen were fitting the *boulangerie* kitchen with Émilie supervising, now that the sale of the old *boulangerie* was moving along. Finally, at the edge of the *étang* he spied his friend. Simon was throwing yesterday's stale croissants to the geese, and Philippe came and stood with him.

'They will get very fat,' he commented shortly.

'I hate geese,' Simon confided. 'Bloody aggressive things, and *loud*. I'm going to have them killed for Christmas, if you'd like one one? Then in spring I'm going to get a few white ducks. I've always fancied ducks,' he said, throwing the last of the croissants at them.

Philippe put his hand on Simon's arm, 'Come for a coffee, I want to talk to you.'

***

The two friends crossed the road, and were soon sitting in the shade of the *Salamandre* sipping the strong black coffee in friendly silence.

'I am going to retire,' Philippe eventually announced. 'I will arrange a long holiday with Josiane, and when we return, I will have forgotten all about recent events.'

'Where will you go?'

'Josiane has been nagging to go visit her sister down in the Lot, and then I think Paris for a week, to do the tourist thing. Then perhaps a river cruise – who knows?'

He played with the teaspoon in the empty cup, leaning forward suddenly, 'I just need to get away for a while, you understand? I remember Jacques Bordes at school. He was a year or two older than me; a misfit and *nasty*. But he and I have both lived in this village and I have known him all my life. He did not have a great life and much of the fault was not his. I'm not excusing him, you understand. He took a different path from the rest of us, and has been punished.'

It was difficult for Philippe to explain, and Simon listened. Never having known Jacques he could only remember the envy and that all-consuming desire for the fairy tale of gold at the mill. Philippe sat back, and Simon waited. Was there going to be more soul-searching?

'How much is this new *chambre* and bathroom going to cost me?' Philippe finally asked.

Simon threw his head back and laughed, 'She's been very

208

restrained, you know! I think you'll be pleased when it's done, and it *will* be finished soon. The floors are good, and I've replaced the old pipes in the bathroom and put a new shower cubicle in – *much* nicer. I think you will get change back from 3000 euros.'

Philippe allowed a small smile to play on his lips, 'She's a good wife. I will tell her it's for her Christmas. Let's see how that goes down. Once she's shouted and thrown something at me, I'll tell her about the holiday. How is *your* romance going? Who wears the trousers in *your* house?'

'Oh, she's had *far* too much independence! And thinks I know nothing; although my French is improving every day. It's all going well. My divorce is done; I'm just waiting for the final papers, and she is impatient for hers, but we've decided *not* to get married. She has decided it's *not* necessary, so I'll just do what she wants.'

'There is a lot to be said for a quiet life,' Philippe agreed, and they walked back to the *moulin*.

***

At the end of the investigation concerning the tragic accident and death of Jacques Bordes, the authorities; through the *mairie*, allowed Simon to recommence the renovations. Whilst the weather was hot and dry, it was decided to fix the loose stones inside the wheel pit, so that when the new wheel was ready to be installed they could do it straight away. So, a waterproof mortar had been prepared and two of the men started to remove, clean and replace any loose stones in the pit, one at either end.

It was on the second day, that the void was found, behind three loosely fitting granite setts near the top of the pit. Émilie made them stop work, and waited till Simon returned from Sarlat, where he had been ordering signs for the new *boulangerie*. The minute he drove into the yard he knew something had happened. The men were all grinning and Émilie was positively bouncing with impatience and delight.

'Have we won the lotto?' he asked as he got out the car.

'Better, I think,' she kissed his cheek and dragged him to the wheel pit.

'Jump in.' she ordered.

Simon looked at her as if she was demented, 'Not in these trousers,' he said shaking his head.

'*Jump* in!' She ordered, 'You won't care about the dirt when you see.'

He climbed down the awaiting ladder whilst Émilie and the men all stood, smiling or grinning, waiting impatiently.

Then he saw the void, and put his hand in. His fingertips touched something that wasn't stone. Cloth of some sort, he imagined with growing excitement. He managed to get his fingers round it and pulled gently, and then realised he was feeling a flat round shape through the cloth. *Surely not!* He looked up to the men, who cheered, and realised he was grinning himself.

In his hand was a very old scrap of hessian or jute. He unfolded the cloth as carefully as his trembling hands allowed and inside lay three gold Napoleons, a couple of badly tarnished silver coins and a small gold finger ring with a tiny red stone. Simon's eyes opened wide with shock and delight. So the story of the gold hidden at the *moulin* was *true* after all!

***

Later, at the *maire's* office, when the treasure lay on the central table and the champagne had finally all been drunk and the archaeologist from Périgueux had been and gone, Georges and Simon simply sat and stared at it. Everyone else had gone home.

'A couple of gold coins and an old ring worth less than 200 euros. That madman Jacques tried to kill you and killed himself for that!' Georges finally said with a sigh.

Simon shrugged.

'What will you do now, after all this, my friend? Will you return to England?'

Simon shook his head. 'This is my *home*. St Honoré came to my rescue when I needed a new start; I can't leave after that. I have good friends here, and despite the actions of *one* person, I'm happy here. Émilie and I will eventually get married and have a family, when she gets used to the idea. I will finish working on the *moulin*, whenever *that* will happen, and I'm proud of the work that I, and the workmen have put in to rescue her. I want to remain here and be part of the next chapter of history. Meantime, I've got some money coming to me and might take some time out to learn how to fish with Philippe. Thankfully, my adventure didn't end that awful night with *my* murder at the *moulin*. I'm looking forward to seeing what new surprises France has in store for me.'

www.ingramcontent.com/pod-product-compliance
Lightning Source LLC
Chambersburg PA
CBHW011036190726
48290CB00011B/2880